THE *way* WE FIGHT

To those who helped me fight.

charleigh

MAYBE I SHOULDN'T HAVE HAD sex with the first guy that caught my attention in the hotel bar. Maybe I shouldn't have had that extra shot of courage in the form of tequila and lime. Maybe I shouldn't have even been in New York City for a job interview that I had no shot of getting in the first place.

But I did... all of it.

I had gotten to New York the afternoon before my interview. It felt like a lifetime of waiting in between, but I couldn't risk flying in any later in case there were delays. The job was too important, years in the making.

In order to pass the time, and lower my anxiety, I ended up at the hotel bar, and that was where I saw him. The definition of tall, dark, and handsome. He had a five o'clock shadow that made him look sensual and tempting. His eyes were dark brown, but they still looked like they were glowing against his dark, tanned skin.

He turned his head my way, as if he could sense me staring, but I didn't turn away. I smiled, unbothered by the fact that a stranger caught me eyeing him. I didn't expect him to smile back, or to get up from his lonely corner booth and join me.

But he did.

He walked with confidence, in a tailored suit that bordered on hugging his thighs too tight. I could tell his body was all muscle underneath, and the way he flexed as he adjusted his cuffs made me swoon before we had even spoken a word to one another.

Taking the stool beside me, he introduced himself as Brett. In a panic, I told him my name was Apple. It was the only thing I could think of since I was in the Big Apple. I could have told him the truth, but I got the feeling he didn't tell *me* the truth, and fair was fair.

Our conversation was casual as I told him I was there for a job interview, and he told me he was there in meetings all day, which had put him in a bad mood. Neither of us asked for details since we knew it didn't really matter. We weren't exchanging numbers or locations, or taking the spark we had with us when we left New York.

But we decided to take it back to his room. What could it hurt? I was in my mid-thirties, supported myself, and went after what I wanted. Strong, independent, and I had no problem following a man back to his room if he could fulfill the promises he whispered in my ear that night.

"I bet I can make you come in seconds."

"I wonder what you taste like, Apple."

"I want to hear you breathing my name in my ear when I make you come."

"You're not going to be able to move after I'm finished with you."

He made good on every promise, and then some. I had never had a night that dirty, that passionate, and that sexually emotional, in my life. Brett made me want to cry with how good he made me feel, making me come more times than I could count, and always ready for another round when I was.

Against the windows, in the shower, against the door, in the bed, on the floor. I got hot just thinking about that night.

And I thought about it all the time. Too much. To the point

that I wasn't sure anyone would ever live up to the fantasy that Brett and I lived.

It had been three months. I was back in Atlanta, inside my small apartment, with my jaw dropped open and regret seeping through me faster than Eminem hitting the second verse in *Godzilla*. I broke into a sweat and started pacing as the TV in my living room blared on and on about how the Atlanta Jets were aiming at another Super Bowl-winning season.

None of that bothered me, of course. It would have been too simple only to be worried about my hometown team's ability to win the Super Bowl. Instead, I was eyeing the man being interviewed.

"Coach," the interviewer said. *"What do you think is the main thing the Jets need to focus on to get back into contention this year?"*

"We need to make sure our quarterback is protected, first and foremost. We have the best quarterback in the league, but he's only one man. The line has to step up and give him time to throw the ball. We also need to make sure our receivers and tight ends have their gloves on. Too many balls are slipping through their fingers this preseason."

"What about the changes the league has made here in Atlanta? Assigning a female referee to work primarily in your home stadium?"

"I think it's great. It shows a lot of evolution for the league. I know she won't be the first in the league, but we are excited to have the expansion of female referees on the field here in Atlanta. We're thankful we have a facility that can accommodate the growth and changes."

"Speaking of growth and changes, this is your fourth season as a head coach. You have a few Super Bowls under your belt and have proven that you can succeed. Yet, everyone questions the fact that you're only forty years old. You always have something to prove."

"Yeah, I do. But I thrive on that pressure. Let them keep second-guessing me..."

I zoned out of the interview after that. I didn't care what else he had to say. I was sure it was all professional and concise. I was sure his words were everything the world wanted to hear.

With his suit and tie on, his hair freshly cut, and the way his lips quirked up before answering each question, the world may not have actually cared what he had to say. At least, not anyone who was attracted to perfection. Coach Levi Peyton looked like he had just stepped out of a magazine ad, and no one should be blamed for having a visceral reaction to him.

Not even me.

Like that one time.

When I met him in New York and he told me his name was Brett. The tequila and tailored suit making him hard to recognize.

His words crept back into my brain as his voice still played on my TV. The man knew how to talk, all right. I never stood a chance once he leaned into me and whispered in my ear all the things he wanted to do to me. Had I known who he was at the time, I would have refrained. In fact, I would have run far, far away. But a hook-up while in New York, with someone I would never see again, seemed like a good idea at the time.

Now, what was I facing?

I got the job I applied for in New York, and Coach Peyton and I were about to be spending a lot of time with one another. And once I made that realization, my first instinct was to call and quit. There was no way I could work beside the man that still made my panties wet when I thought about his deep, commanding voice.

But there was a focus on my role, and it would make headlines if I bailed.

Because I was *that* female referee. The one poised to make history.

For the last three months, I had been holed up in a training facility, working beyond comprehension while getting doubted by my peers. I had to put in extra work to be taken seriously. I was being presented with the opportunity of a lifetime, and would be a fool to let it go and let the sins of my past win.

There was also a chance Coach Peyton wouldn't even recognize me. It wasn't like I planned on wearing my sexy dress and stilettos onto the field. My hair wouldn't be done up, and I was only allowed to wear very basic makeup.

The complete opposite of who he met in New York.

So, I was doing it.

I would be there every chance I got and prove to everyone that the NFL was moving in a positive direction. No matter how hard I had to fight.

levi

THE PRESSURE WAS MOUNTING.

Every year seemed to get worse and worse.

I had been hired as one of the youngest head coaches in the NFL ever, and four years later, that label was still ringing in my ears every day. Who cared if I was young? I had led the Jets to Super Bowls and would do it again.

Yet, everyone waited for me to fail.

The media was what drove that narrative. They wanted *that* story. My fall from grace. It's what happens when you become the best. You became a target. It was me against everyone else.

Unless I failed, no one else could win.

It was fucking exhausting and stressful.

It was also isolating.

My entire job was lonely.

During the season, I practically lived at the practice complex, and in the stadium. The only people who came to me were the ones who needed something. Football was all I thought about, and even though I loved the game more than anything, I was reaching a point where it felt like I had peaked.

"Knock, knock." I looked up to see Cam Nichols, my prized quarterback, standing in the doorway to my office. "Lost in thought, Coach?"

"Pretty much. What's up?" I waved him in.

"Nothing really. Just headed home to my girl and passed by. Looked like you needed me to check on you."

I laughed and leaned back in my chair. "Ready for Sunday?"

"Deflecting?"

"Probably. But I still want to know."

"More than ready, Coach. The first game of the preseason always feels good. And with Black finally catching the ball like he used to, my arm is anxious to throw his way."

Ty Black was our number one tight end, but the start to his season had been rocky. I sent him to ballet lessons on a whim during camp, and it worked. Another feather in my head coaching cap. I felt ballet lessons for professional football players would soon become a trend. They may even call it the "Peyton method."

I laughed at the thought and turned my attention back to Cam. "Good. Enjoy your day off, I'll see you at the team hotel Saturday night."

"You got it, Coach." Cam smirked and backed out of my office.

Jealousy rose up in me as I thought about him going home to his girlfriend, the comfort of knowing he wasn't alone and had someone waiting for him. Two someone's, really, since he and his best friend were with the same girl.

Turning my chair around, I thought about the last time I was with someone. What started as a bad day had ended up being the best night of my fucking life and probably the reason I was in a three-month dry spell. No one seemed likely to compare to the woman I met in New York on my shitty business trip.

Apple Parks.

I knew that wasn't her real name. The fact that we were in the

Big Apple near Central Park was my first clue, along with the way she said, "Ummm, Apple?" when I asked what her name was. I didn't mind, though. In fact, I loved playing the anonymity game.

Hell, I started it.

Groaning in the quiet space of my office, I thought back on the way her skin pinked under every touch. I had never had a woman that responsive, nor one who made me feel that hard just by looking at her. I spotted her in the hotel bar as I tried to drown out the meetings I had earlier that day with liquor and peanuts. But instead of my planned twelve shots and straight-to-bed method, I saw her and decided a night with her would be a better cure.

Her long brown hair, the way her brown eyes matched mine with a glint in them. She was shorter than I was, but I could tell by her toned arms that she was a force. Maybe even a fighter like me.

One night was all I ever had time to give, and I wanted to give it to her. We shared a night I had obsessed over since.

By the time I woke up, she had left my room, and it was the first time I was actually disappointed not to see my one-night stand still lingering in the morning. It was just as well, though, because I hopped on my flight home that day and got back to my lonely reality.

But fuck, sometimes I closed my eyes and used my memories of that night to take the edge off. I knew I was about to have one of those nights, and as sick and perverse as it sounded, I looked forward to my alone time in the shower with the vision of her lips wrapped around me.

No media, no players, no owners, no other coaches... just me and whatever I had time to think about as the water hit my shoulders.

I swiveled back around to face my desk and turned my

computer off. I didn't bother packing anything to take home. I knew I was going to be right back in that office the next morning. Even though the players had time off, I didn't, and until the season was over, I probably wouldn't.

As I walked down the dark hallway of the offices, my phone rang.

"Yeah?" I answered, almost annoyed.

"Hey Levi, it's Art, how are ya?"

I stopped in my tracks, the voice of the NFL's commissioner, Art Mixon, deep and stern in my ear. He insisted on first names and friendship, but I also understood that he was the reason I had been in New York three months ago. The owner of the Jets, Richard Elder, and I were summoned to his office for a meeting about etiquette regarding the new female referee we would have in Atlanta.

"Yes sir. I'm well, how are you?"

"Good, good. Listen, I just wanted to check in personally, make sure everything was ready for Sunday."

"Have you talked to Richard about that? It's all I can do to make sure my team is ready. I haven't thought anymore about the distractions we will be having."

As shitty as it sounded, making special exceptions for a female referee was a distraction. We already had vultures in Atlanta, after me, and a story. They were going to be ten times worse as they chased down the chance to either praise or ruin the poor girl who took the job. Was I supposed to be responsible for that, too?

"Of course I have. He said the facilities were ready, and the team had been warned that there would be extra eyes on them this year as the world tuned in to see how Ms. Wright did."

From what they told me, Ms. Wright was fairly young and a whiz when it came to the game. She passed her interview and training with flying colors, and they were excited to see the game expanding. Honestly, from what they said, she sounded like she could handle herself and didn't need me to worry about anything.

"Look, I get that you're concerned about how this all plays out. But it's unprofessional for me to look after a referee. If she applied for the job and got hired, then I'm sure she can handle it. If she can't, she shouldn't do this job, end of story. She's a referee. We are not supposed to be friendly with the officials."

"Oh shit, Levi," Art laughed. "I don't want you to wine and dine her. I just want to make sure she has appropriate space to change and escape to. We can't have her in the same locker room as the other officials, and Atlanta is one of the few teams that has the space. Richard was all too excited to help us out, and I am sure he wants things to be smooth. But I also need to make sure the image of the NFL stays on the positive side, as well."

I pushed the exit doors open and clicked for the automatic start on my car to engage. "Well then, I think you have everything handled, sir. I'll be there coaching my ass off, and Ms. Wright has a private room for her locker space. Let's hope she calls a good game." I knew that was the truth because it was down the same corridor the home team came in and out of. But I also felt sorry for her. If she didn't call a good game, Richard would be her worst nightmare. He had already told me as much.

Honestly, Richard's interest in her was more than Art bargained for, but that wasn't my business. I tried to convince myself not to care.

"Oh, she will," he assured me. "And the entire world will be watching."

The media would be crazed if they knew what went on behind the scenes to make sure everything was just right when the cameras rolled. It was almost embarrassing how much the NFL focused on the production of everything besides the game.

I wasn't going to let it be my focus, though. The team and my guys were the only things I cared about, and after being analyzed and prodded about whether I could sustain our championships, I knew the season was going to be rough.

Add in a new referee that the league wanted to coddle–and Richard wanted to control–and I knew I had a fight on my hands.

charleigh

I WAS in my black and white stripes with my hair pulled into a braid under my black cap. Walking down the corridor of the stadium toward the field with my fellow officials was a high. I was the only female, and the youngest by a long shot, at thirty-five years old. But the guys I was teamed up with seemed like amazing guys to be working with. We felt like a team.

The head referee, Martin, was a fit sixty-year-old man who could have been my dad. He had more experience than the rest of us, hence being the head ref, and was in charge as long as we were a unit on the field.

The big LJ on my back indicated that I was the line judge, and that was where I would be the entire season. Along the sidelines, marking downs, throwing flags, and responding to the Coach's requests for timeouts.

That was where my problems started. Because as the line judge, I would be primarily on the home side of the field, giving Coach Peyton a better chance of recognizing me as the girl who sucked his dick like a Slurpee and bailed from the room while he slept, never to be seen again.

I should have quit.

Instead, I held my head high and walked onto the field to a chorus of boos.

"Don't worry, we always get yelled at. Fans hate the refs."

"That's comforting," I deadpanned.

That wasn't my first time on the football field. I wasn't just a football fan with uncanny knowledge and a drive to be near the field. I had been officiating football games at the college level for five years. But things worked differently in college. Not to mention, I had never officiated a high-level college.

The officiating crew did our normal pregame rituals of small talk and handshakes, and I met some people along the sidelines who congratulated me for my role. The players were warming up, and the coaches were swarming, but everything seemed to settle and move smoothly, allowing me to breathe easier before game time.

It was preseason, and that made the air lighter as everyone was excited to start the season on a good foot. I was thankful for the preseason games, not only for the players, but for me, because I was realizing that those games would help me get used to the goings-on before things got serious.

Or so I thought.

Once I hit the sideline and the game started, I had chills racing through me, and I knew it wasn't the adrenaline from the game. It was because I was standing in front of Coach Peyton. I was paying attention to the game, but I could hear his voice behind me. He was calling plays, yelling, and walking down the field with me as the ball moved back and forth.

Right before halftime, I threw my first flag for pass interference, and even though it was undoubtedly pass interference, I heard Coach Peyton yell, "Are you blind?"

I ignored his anger and referred to my fellow referees, who also confirmed they saw pass interference, and the call was announced. When I walked back to the sideline, I kept my head down until I could turn around and face the field again.

The entire experience was awkward.

I was balancing being anonymous with being taken seriously, while also battling the weakness in my knees from hearing his deep voice again. His words came in behind me like they did that night in New York, when he grabbed my hair from behind and told me he was going to spank my ass.

My body shook and I had to tap my head to get it out of that hotel room and back onto the field. By that time, I could hear Coach Peyton behind me, yelling. He was telling me I was blind as a bat and missed the call, but I had no clue what had even happened.

Was there a play?

Did they throw it near me?

Was I supposed to make a call?

I knew I was in the wrong somehow, but I held my own, determined to keep moving along the sidelines like I knew what to do, and not let him know that I probably missed the call. Thankfully, by the time the next play went on, he had found something else to yell about that didn't involve me.

When halftime started, I got to head into my own personal room where I was safe from eyes and ears. I ran alongside my fellow referees and into the tunnel where they quickly turned into their locker room, away from mine.

I was alone for two full minutes as I walked to the area they showed me was exclusively mine, before someone slid in step beside me.

"You need to keep your eyes on the fucking play," Coach Peyton's voice boomed angrily. "This is preseason, so a lot gets overlooked, but if this were a regular season game, your ass would be out the door already."

I nodded, not wanting to voice my opinion, or show him my

face. I was so completely overwhelmed and anxious that I felt lightheaded and was on the verge of showing myself to the door.

Once he was done saying his peace, he jogged past me, and farther down the corridor to the locker room, while I took a left into a small hallway that held my quarters. I opened the door quickly and slammed it behind me, turning the lock so that no one dared to come in.

It was a small space, but there had been a good-sized locker installed, a dinette-style table, a small fridge, and a leather couch. Off to the side was a bathroom and a huge shower that, though big, looked to have been installed as an afterthought.

I plopped onto the soft leather and bit my lip to keep from screaming. There was no way I could eat during our short break since I was already on the verge of vomiting.

Up in the corner, a small TV with the broadcast of the game was on. The volume was too low to hear, but there I was, on repeat, being discussed. Probably mentioning my missed call, or how silly I looked out there. I was only 5'4, and standing next to the huge players and coaches, I bet I looked ridiculous.

Fragile.

I never felt inadequate in my life. I had always been tough as nails–mentally and physically. Even without the fact that I had a one-night stand with Coach Peyton, I still would have felt small.

My brother, Jesse, and my mom were the only people in my life who believed I could actually make it in the world of professional football. When I finally realized one day I would never be big enough to play, I decided I wanted to referee. Mom and Jesse bought me my first study book by selling extra crafts at the flea market where they worked.

They worked hard for that $30, and I told them I wouldn't let them down, that I would do it. I had finally made it, and I knew they had a TV set up at the market to watch me officiate my first pro game.

That reminder made me stand as tall as I could and march toward my small fridge. I gulped a bottle of water and then headed out onto the field to finish the game and make them proud.

Who cared if I'd slept with the coach? That was done and over, and he was equally responsible for that misdemeanor. We'd had no idea who each other was, and we would just have to live with brushing our secret under the rug. I bet Coach Peyton didn't want anyone knowing, either.

He had enough to deal with on his own. We both had a lot of pressure. We both had a reason to keep our secret.

So, who cared if he saw my face and realized who I was? So what if he didn't like the calls I made on the field?

We both had jobs to do, and I was going to do it well.

levi

IT REALLY DIDN'T MATTER that we were playing a preseason game. To a coach, they were all important and meaningful. Especially one being scrutinized for every decision.

Ms. Wright better have been glad I was feeling extra tense myself, and didn't care to engage more than I had. I just warned her she needed to get it together, and quickly, which was not done from the goodness of my heart. More like a warning that I could fight a bigger fight if she made me.

And I wasn't even the worst of her problems.

By the time I got back onto the field for the second half, my mind was back in the game and I was running through the motions. Once again I was behind Ms. Wright as she called a fairly good second half as the line judge.

With twenty seconds left on the clock, at the end of the game, she spotted the ball an inch too short, in my opinion, and I finally lost it on her again.

"Are you fucking kidding me, lady?"

"Quiet down, Coach," she warned. "You have a red flag if you want to challenge it."

"I'm not wasting my red flag," I yelled at the back of her head.

"You're going to get the calls right, or shit is going to get ugly like I warned you it would."

For the first time since the game started, she flipped around and stared me in the eyes. It was my first good look at her, and I was not prepared for the woman looking back at me.

Brown hair, dark brown eyes, flush cheekbones, and familiar lips. Those lips started to snarl at me and she got closer.

"Is that a threat, Coach?"

I was stunned silent, her voice bringing back memories of the night I thought about more often than I should have. "Apple?"

Her eyes widened, shocked at the name I used, and probably equally shocked I recognized her so immediately. *Like I could ever forget that mouth.*

"Watch how you talk to me, Coach. We are all being watched. You wouldn't want to have to deal with more shit than you can handle."

Her teeth were clenched as she spoke, her lips barely moving. She was well aware that cameras were everywhere, but I seemed to have forgotten because I reached out to touch her on instinct and that was a big problem.

"Don't touch me, either. You better get yourself in check, now."

She turned and waved to the head official that I wasn't challenging the call, and the game moved forward. If it hadn't been for the guys celebrating around me, I wouldn't have even known we had won. I was too stunned to make any calls or decisions after locking eyes with Apple.

Or whatever her real name was.

Ms. Wright.

After shaking hands with the other coach, I ran from the field as if I had a meeting I was about to miss, and hid in my office until someone came to force me to speak to the media.

After I met with the media, I started pacing my office again. I had locked the door so no one would bother me, completely unable to get my head out of whatever the hell was happening. Apple was there. She was the new referee. She was the one I was going to have to be standing behind all year and trying not to throw my clipboard at.

Did she know who I was when we met?

Did she sleep with me thinking it would help her get the job?

Did she not realize I had no say so in the matter?

Did she realize the shit she had gotten herself into?

After I was sure everyone else had left, I grabbed my jacket and headed to the parking lot. I needed a shower. Ten minutes of total peace. But I was not going to think about New York.

Fuck no.

It was wrong on so many levels to be jerking my dick to the image of the new referee on her knees in front of me.

"Fuck," I yelled into the parking garage, letting the word echo to remind me how fucked up it all was.

I stomped like a kid having a tantrum, and I wasn't even sure what my main issue was. Was I mad she lied to me? Was I mad she was going to distract me all season? Was I mad there was going to be an awkward aura around us, making my life hell?

I wasn't completely sure, but I wasn't in the right headspace to be dealing with it either. So, when I turned the corner to where I parked my car and saw Ms. Wright unlocking her own car, it was all I could do to stop walking and back away.

I didn't make it far, though, as she looked up and saw me. Her eyes widened, much like they had on the field earlier, and I could no longer walk backward. The anger and mixed emotions coursing through me were all leading me straight to her.

She closed her car door without getting in and crossed her arms, readying herself for the fight she knew we were about to have. I'd give her credit. She looked like a formidable opponent as she cocked her head to the side and waited for me to get closer.

"What the fuck?" was all I could say. It was the only thing I could think of to start the conversation.

"Honestly, Coach, this hasn't been fun for me either."

"You trying to tell me you planned all this?"

She uncrossed her arms and stood taller. She was no longer in her uniform. Instead, she was in tight jeans and a black top that wrapped around her body and dipped low over the top of her tits. Her hair was wet and put up into a messy twist on her head.

"You are not implying that I spent the night with you knowing this would happen, are you?"

"You think I could help you out? Sleep your way to the sideline?"

I barely got the words out before she took her right hand and planted it across my face. "Don't you dare imply that I whored myself to you for a job. I had no idea who the fuck you were until a few days ago."

"And you chose to be on the field for your big reveal? Hoping I got caught with my pants down?"

"I'm not doing this with you. I didn't plan this, I don't look forward to it, and I wish to God I could quit. But you and I both know I can't, so we are just going to have to deal with it."

"You can start by keeping your hands off my face." I leaned in closer to her, trying to intimidate her, but she never backed away.

"Then I would be careful what you call me, and what you imply about me. Not only to my face, but to anyone."

"You think I want anyone to know about this?"

"I hope not, but I can't control what you do."

I backed away and started walking toward my car without another word. I wasn't going to reassure her that my lips were sealed. I mean, they sure as fuck were, but I wasn't going to give her the satisfaction.

When I got in my car, I slammed my hand onto my steering wheel and sat there, running my emotions through my head.

I honestly thought if I ever saw her again, I would smile, remember how much fun we had, and invite her for another round. I lived the last three months with the memory of how perfect that night was, and it kept me grounded when the stress seemed to be too much.

It was easy to use her because I knew I would never see her again. She was safe to fantasize about, safe to escape inside of my head as the world around me tried to tear me down.

Now that she was right in front of me again, my first words were hateful. The impact of what it all meant for me–that my memory was now a nightmare, that my career was now in jeopardy, that my remaining sanity was gone–made me shake with the need to hit something.

It had been a few months since I had been to the gym outside of my apartment or the training facilities, but I drove straight there. I needed to put on some gloves, swing at someone as they tried to beat the shit out of me, and hope that it was enough to erase the fight I had in me towards Ms. Wright.

Maybe it was all a coincidence, but that didn't make it easier to handle.

I had a week until the next game, another home game, and I had to face the fact that I had slept with the NFL's coveted female referee. The one thing that brought me peace was that she was in a worse position than I was. I knew she wouldn't tell a soul because she would reap the worst of it, and if it were all truly a coincidence, then she would keep quiet about our tryst in New York, and neither of us would have to worry or think of it again.

charleigh

I WAS ALMOST glad that was over with.

It was bound to happen, and ripping the Band-Aid off at the first game was better than trying to hide all season. I just didn't expect Coach Peyton to be so angry.

Upset? Sure. But he was borderline raging as he approached me in the parking lot. I had almost flinched, scared of what he was capable of since it wasn't like I knew him all that well. But I stood my ground, and hopefully, let him know that I was not a part of some evil plan to bring him down.

If he stayed out of my way, I would stay out of his.

As I started my old red Honda and pulled out of the parking garage, my phone started ringing, and I answered it to a chorus of squeals and screams.

"You did so well, honey!" My mom's voice was high, and she continued to scream in excitement as a smile finally lit my face up.

"I completely zoned out for a minute," I admitted to her. "God, it was so hard."

"But you did it, and after all those years at high schools and colleges, getting talked down to because you wanted to be on the field, you finally made it where you wanted to be."

Tears sprung in my eyes, and her words reminded me once again why I couldn't quit. I had spent my entire adult life preparing for the day I got to be an NFL referee. It wasn't magic and luck that led me to New York three months ago, it was hard work and determination.

Sacrifice.

People thought I was completely nuts to want to be an NFL official. Why would anyone want to subject themselves to that sort of beratement and scrutiny? Those people just didn't understand how much I loved the game. And most people never got my full story. I stopped trying to explain myself years ago.

"Come over for dinner, we can celebrate!"

"Oh, Mom, I want to do that so bad, but I have to head home. I still have to work in the morning."

"Seems so unfair that you finally landed your dream job and you still have to work."

I snorted because it was true. But the NFL didn't give me a full-time contract. Since I was only traveling in a limited capacity and still in a probationary period, the money I made at games wasn't going to cut it year-round. I had no choice but to keep my original job so that I could pay my bills. But being a trainer at the gym near my house was a good gig, and I had been there for years now. Leaving that job was never something I wanted to consider, and my boss was more than supportive of me pursuing officiating.

"I don't mind, Mom. You know Bobby is good to me there."

"Yeah well, he better be."

"I'll come by after work and help with the crafts for a bit," I offered. I knew that would make Mom happy, even if I didn't want to spend my evenings twisting tulle.

"I'll cook something, and we can make a night of it."

"Okay, Mom, sounds good," I added before ending the call.

I held back my groan, already regretting my offer. I hated arts and crafts, but I loved spending time with my mom, so if she wanted to make a night of it, I would. I may have to spend some extra time at the gym to compensate, though.

I started going to Bobby's gym as a way to work out my aggression. Our little family had been dealt a shitty hand once my dad died, and sometimes I was angry that life for us couldn't have been easier.

Mom did her best as a single parent, working every job she could, and selling her crafts at the local flea market on the weekends. I helped her and Jesse for a while, but eventually, Bobby offered me a job, and I took it. He was about the age my dad would have been, and ended up being like the dad I never had.

I was thankful for Bobby, not only for my job but for how he invited Jesse into the fold as well. Jesse had always had a harder time because he wasn't very social. He was diagnosed with autism in his teens, and lived at home with Mom, but he would go to the gym with me, where he felt safe.

Bobby had him in a boxing ring in no time, and it became a coping mechanism that Jesse still used when he was feeling especially overwhelmed. He could put headphones on, focus on one person, and swing his arms until he was exhausted. It gave him confidence, and even though he would probably always live with Mom, he was more fulfilled individually.

Whatever my future held with the NFL, I would always remain faithful to Bobby, and the guys I worked with.

"Hey yo!" Bobby yelled as I walked into work the following morning.

"Hey, yo, yourself," I yawned.

"I saw my girl making those calls yesterday. How did it feel? Tell me everything."

I looked around the lobby of the gym, which mostly consisted of old chairs and a ragged wooden counter with marker and pen marks all over it. Bobby and two of the other guys who worked with me, Bond and Axton, sat in the old chairs looking at me.

"It was good. I mean, what do you want to know?"

"I want to know what you were thinking about when you blew that call," Bond teased. "No, wait. You didn't blow it; you didn't even see it."

I had avoided the sports news because I knew that would be mentioned, but I should have been more prepared to face the Neanderthal I worked with.

"Hey, lay off," Bobby interjected. "You did good, kid."

My heart warmed at how he called me "Kid," even though I wasn't a kid. Bond and Axton were the kids–both twenty-seven but acted seventeen. "Thanks, Bobby."

I looked over at my coworkers, who were still smirking at me while also biting their cheeks. I couldn't help but laugh. They wanted to tease me so bad, but knew Bobby would send them home early if they gave me too much shit. So, I smirked right back and headed into the women's locker room to get ready for my day.

Throughout the day, I pounded the ring hard, sparring with some clients, and then helping a few on the machines in the other part of the gym. None of the clientele knew I had blown a call. None of them even cared because they didn't know I was officiating. Most of the people who came to our gym were low-income folks who spent more time working than they did watching football.

By the time the day ended, I had almost forgotten about my

other life. I was calmer and content. It was as if the drama of the day before hadn't happened, and I was right back in the swing of normalcy.

Then I saw Coach Peyton at a press conference on the TV as I walked into the lobby to leave for the day, and Bond turned the volume up so we could all hear.

"What are your feelings on the new referee? How did she call the game?"

He licked his lips and popped his back, tapping his fingers on the podium and trying to think of how he was going to answer. I was frozen, watching what he would say, almost expecting him to spill his disdain for me.

"In every new situation, there's a learning curve. This isn't just preseason for us. It is for the officials as well. I think Ms. Wright will settle in and do as well as anyone else in the league. I doubt she wants all the focus on her, though, just because of her gender."

My heart was beating fast, and I almost teared up at his words. They were perfect, and deflected from any smearing he could have chosen to do at that moment. He also mentioned not wanting the attention because of my gender, and he was right. I didn't want to be differentiated where the job was concerned.

Pulling my bag up onto my shoulder, I chanced a look at the guys who I thought were still watching the TV, but they weren't. Their eyes were on me, and I knew they saw me blush at Coach's words.

I didn't give them time to tease me again, though. I walked onto the street and headed toward my old car. Mom didn't live far, so I made it to her house in no time, and began the mundane task of cutting twelve-inch strips of tulle for a wreath she was making.

Jesse was in his room, so it was just us on the floor of the living room as we chatted about how our days had been. Mom didn't immediately ask me about the game, probably knowing I didn't want to talk about it based on how the news kept analyzing the one fucking play I wasn't watching.

But just like everyone else, curiosity got the best of her as well.

"Why did you space out during the game?" Mom asked. "It's all over the news."

"Ugh..." was my first reply before adding, "It was new. Exciting. The moment got the best of me."

"I get it," Mom said sweetly, not even looking up from where she twisted her tulle. "Just remember to stay focused, honey. This is the big time. You will be scrutinized for every move you make."

"I know, Mom. I was prepared for that, and I will handle it. Officiating isn't new. I've had shit thrown at my car before by angry fans, remember? That division two college took their games seriously."

"I remember," Mom huffed. "But you got that call right. This one, you were wrong."

"Gee, thanks."

Mom laughed, and I threw the tulle I had cut at her. It didn't matter how old I got, I was always her child, and she was always going to be my mom. She had become my best friend over the years–my only friend–and a part of me wanted to tell her the truth.

Sex wasn't off the table when it came to my mom. We'd talked about it since I was fifteen. She knew when I lost my virginity, and to whom. She knew the guys I had dated, and the ones who stayed over at my house. She knew it all.

But I never told her about New York. Maybe because it was out of the ordinary for me. I have had my share of one-night stands, but none with a stranger, using fake names. Especially none that ended up being a conflict of interest where my career was concerned.

I wanted to tell her, though. I needed to tell someone.

But just as I opened my mouth, Jesse walked into the room,

and I closed back up. I definitely didn't need my younger brother to know about my sex life. That was a hard pass for me. So, I let it go for the night and tried to focus on family time, the food Mom had made, and all the stories Jesse wanted to tell me about the flea market.

BY THE END of the week, I was so focused on coaching that I had almost forgotten about the fact that I had to face "Apple" again.

That was a lie. I didn't forget.

In fact, I thought about it constantly. I could never figure out why I stayed so angry, though. Other than the added stress I was under, knowing my one-night stand was calling my games. Still, it seemed like it was something I should have been able to look past.

But I couldn't.

When asked about it in the media, I tried to be as politically correct as I could, but deep down, I wanted to demand she leave so that my life would be easier. Even if that was selfish, I needed a fucking break.

Friday was spent answering questions about whether I would even have a win at all if it weren't for our star quarterback. How many ways could I say, "I guess we'll never know?"

Saturday was spent locked in my hotel room, watching movies and Googling Ms. Wright. Her real name was Charleigh Wright. She grew up in Atlanta and had over ten years of officiating experience. There wasn't much on her personal life, but since she sat on my face in New York, I was assuming she was single.

Although, who knows for sure anymore? Not to mention, it had been three months since that night, and she could very well be in a relationship now.

"Fuck!" I yelled and threw my phone onto the floor to keep myself from looking for more. Charleigh Wright was "Apple" and she needed to stay that way. I needed to stop thinking about New York.

I looked over to the window of the hotel I was in with the team and thought about having her against the window in New York overlooking the Hudson River. Her tits were pressed to the cold glass, and I fucked her from behind while I told her everyone could see her, could see us. She squeezed me so tight and came, almost falling from the window and onto the floor.

I reached down and squeezed my dick that instantly got hard every time I thought about that night. Then I let go and pounded my fist into the bed. That was definitely my problem.

That night had been one of the best of my life, and I used that night when I needed to escape. Now, that was no longer possible. I had to forget it all happened, and I didn't want to. I still needed that escape.

I got up from the bed and decided to get dressed. I never, ever, spent the night before a game trying to fuck someone, and especially never in Atlanta. But I was desperate to fuck Charleigh from my memory. She was the last person I had been with, and I reasoned that it would be therapeutic to let that go and be with someone else.

When I got down to the lobby, I was relieved that no players were mingling around. They didn't need to see me like that.

Instead of staying in the hotel, I walked a few blocks to a bar I knew the guys frequented, but wouldn't be there tonight. The 678 Bar was a high-class dive bar, always busy, with a decent clientele, live club music on some nights, and the feel of walking into a dive bar. It was unique, and I instantly felt at ease as I sidled up to the bar.

"What'll it be?" a large man about my own age, asked me.

"Scotch, neat."

"You got it boss." I almost flinched at his words because I was used to being called boss, and I wondered if that meant he recognized me. But when he called the guy next to me "boss" as well, I relaxed again.

I looked around, hoping to find someone I could take back to the hotel with me. Or even just the bathroom.

Most of the time, women flocked to me. I knew I was no slouch. I was tall, built, charming, and old enough to let women know they had just met a man, not a boy. Being with women was never hard for me.

Once I locked eyes with a tall blonde, gave her a smirk, and nodded toward the dance floor, I knew the night was going to be cake. I hated dancing, *fuck* I hated dancing. But it was a turn-on for women and made my life easier.

Apple didn't want to dance, I thought to myself before squashing that thought away. I was on a mission to fuck her out of my system before the game. Thinking of her wasn't going to work.

"Hey," the girl squeaked, running a hand down my arm. "New here?"

"Just in town for the night," I smiled as we started to move together.

"What's your name?"

"Bre...Brent." Brett was my go-to, but even that reminded me of New York, so I made up a new name on the spot. "What's yours?"

"Molly," she giggled. "I actually work here."

Fuck, that was both inconvenient and convenient at the same

time. It meant I could never go back, but also meant she would know where the quickest place to escape to would be.

"Night off, and you're here?"

"Sorta," she shrugged. "I got off an hour ago and needed to let loose before I head home."

"Convenient to work and play in the same place."

"Very," she purred into my ear.

We were close, moving to the beat of a song I didn't recognize. I knew then and there that Molly was beyond perfect. She was hanging around 678 for the same thing I was–sex. So, I decided not to waste our time.

"Where can we go that's more private?" I ran a hand down her side and slightly kissed her cheek, letting her know my intentions.

"You're making this easy on me," she moaned.

I had never been so satisfied with not having to work for it. I should have been at my hotel preparing for the game, so the quicker I got out of that club, the better.

"I'll make it good for you too." I snaked my hand to her jeans-covered ass and squeezed, making her fall into my chest. "Now, tell me where to take you so I can get these off."

She turned and grabbed my hand, leading me to a spiral staircase. I followed her up, wondering if it led to offices or bathrooms. When she opened the door, though, we were on the roof of the building. It was deserted, looking like it was only used for occasional smoke breaks, judging by the piles of cigarette butts sitting around.

"Over here." She pulled me around the corner and to a side of the building where no one would catch us. Her lips found mine, and she tried taking control of what was happening, but that wasn't how I worked.

I was always in control. That was what made me a good coach.

Pushing Molly back against the wall, I separated our lips and shook my head at her, silently tsking at her attempt. "No kissing on the lips."

She smiled big, amused by my words. Probably thinking it was some weird kink I was implementing, when in reality, I hadn't kissed anyone since New York. Even though I wanted to forget that night, I was reminded of how kissing changed the dynamics of what I wanted.

Had I never kissed Apple, maybe I wouldn't still be thinking about her. Maybe I wouldn't have been fazed when I locked eyes with her on that field. Maybe I wouldn't even care.

So, I wouldn't be kissing Molly, or anyone else for that matter. I wasn't risking any more feelings for her, or for me.

"Take your pants down," I told her. "Show me how wet you are."

I knew she would be dripping. She was getting off just on the idea of being fucked. It didn't matter to her what happened as long as she got an orgasm.

She opened her jeans just enough to welcome me in. "Come feel for yourself."

I started to shake my head. I told her to show me, and that was what I expected her to do, but I also realized I wasn't even ready yet. I needed to touch her, get myself into the moment, and get my dick hard so I could go back to my hotel as soon as possible.

"Hands to yourself," I warned her as I got closer. I made eye contact with her and slipped my right hand into her tight jeans. Her panties were soaked, just like I thought they would be. When I bent a finger up to slide it inside of her, she moaned and started to reach for my shoulders. But I quickly took my free hand and held her back.

I started to move, rubbing her clit at the same time I took my finger in and out of her. I added a second finger, and she moaned louder, making me take my free hand from her arms to her mouth.

When I crooked my finger, I could feel her trembling. She had gotten so close, so fast. She knew what she wanted, and I found that incredibly appealing.

Unfortunately, my dick still wasn't stirring.

"Let me feel how hard you are," she begged as I kept moving. But I wasn't fucking hard, and she couldn't know that. She would think I was broken.

Oh fuck, what if I was broken?

I closed my eyes and willed myself to harden. I thought about every sexy woman I had ever been with, every touch I had given. I tried to be in that moment with Molly, getting off on having a stranger on the rooftop of a club, and how exciting it was supposed to be.

But my dick didn't budge.

Not until my mind drifted back to New York. The way Charleigh tilted her head when I walked up to her. The way her smile shot straight to my cock and made me ache before I had ever touched her. I thought about the way she poked my chest playfully as I told her I wanted to take her upstairs to my room.

Only then did I get hard.

But when I opened my eyes and saw Molly staring back at me with a look of lust and yearning, all I wanted to do was leave.

I really was broken.

Instead of sheathing myself with a condom and turning Molly around to fuck her, I just went harder with my hand. I pounded her as hard as I could from the awkward angle and pushed her over the edge before she could stop me.

She screamed my fake name, riding my hand until she had been satisfied. Then I pulled her jeans and took two steps back. Molly followed, attempting to grab my pants once again, but I shook my head.

I couldn't do it, not just physically, but mentally.

Molly saw the look on my face and pulled her jeans back into place. I thought she would be mad, but she smiled at me and grabbed the hand I just had in her pussy.

"She must be special," Molly whispered before taking my fingers into her mouth. I was too stunned to stop her, but she cleaned herself from my fingers and then dropped my hand again. "Thanks for not leaving me hangin'."

I stayed quiet and still as she walked back toward the door we came through. When she was gone and the door slammed shut, I finally turned my head toward the wall. I walked over and looked down, still in some state of shock that I just turned down no-strings sex when I clearly needed out of my head.

The fact that I couldn't get hard without Charleigh in my head had me fucked up. Had it been that bad since I met her? I guess I had no way to know because I hadn't had sex since then. I must have gotten into a habit and was stuck.

"For fuck's sake," I mumbled to myself. "This is so fucked up."

charleigh

SUNDAY'S GAME started off easy.

Coach Peyton stayed away from me during the pregame, and I avoided him as well. I chanced a few glances to see if he was ready to kill me for slapping him the week before, but I assumed he also knew he deserved it.

We were just moving into the second quarter on a hot and sunny day with the dome of the stadium open when I finally gave him something to yell at me about. An unsportsmanlike conduct penalty against Tyson Black, his star tight end.

"Are you kidding me?" He stood next to me and yelled while the players moved on and off the field. "Ninety-nine shoved him down."

"I only saw eighty-two," I responded, referring to Tyson's jersey number. Honestly, calling it like I saw it was my job. If number ninety-nine started it, I didn't see it. And that was okay because I was watching the play. I was doing my job.

Coach Peyton would just have to stand down.

But he didn't.

"Are you fucking blind?" he yelled again. "What were you looking at, the color of your nails?"

His words made me turn red from anger and embarrassment. I put my whistle in my mouth to hide my lip movements from the cameras and turned to him while the play was still halted.

"Are you insinuating I care more about my nails than my job? That's a pretty sexist thing to say."

Coach Peyton wasn't even looking at me, but I watched as he put his play sheet in front of his mouth and unplugged his headset from the pack around his waist.

"I warned you, Apple," he snarled my fake name. "You're gonna regret being a lousy official in the NFL."

Tilting my head a little, I beaded my eyes at him, praying the cameras didn't catch me snarling. "Your dick isn't big enough to get away with acting like an asshole."

His head snapped in my direction at my words, and I gave him one last glare before turning and walking away. If I had a mic, I would have dropped it because the look on his face was better than I could've imagined.

Thankfully, he left me alone after that, and let me get back to work. But the pettiness I felt in my bones stayed intact. That man made me angry, and I had no idea why. Sure, it was well known that coaches and officials didn't see eye to eye, but with him, it felt personal.

It was personal.

Maybe I shouldn't have snuck out. Maybe we should have said goodbye. Would that have made things easier?

Nope, fuck that.

It was a one-night stand, and we weren't supposed to see each other again. There were no reasons for niceties and goodbyes. Plus, I probably would have missed my interview if I had not left while he was sleeping. Because despite being pissed at the man that was currently stalking toward me to call a timeout, I wanted more of him.

"Time out!" he yelled in my direction.

I promptly blew my whistle for the break and let him convene with his team. Without meaning to, I kept my eyes on him as he settled in the middle of the guys.

He was just as tall and built as they were. He wore slim fit, ankle joggers with a Jets logo on the thigh, and it caught my eye. Then he turned, and I was looking at his ass, an ass I admired naked as it walked from the bedroom to dispose of the condoms we used in New York.

I was back there again, lying in bed, watching the way he moved and thinking to myself that he had to be an athlete of some sort. I wasn't completely wrong, and I was willing to bet he played football not so long ago.

Not that I was going to look it up. I didn't want to care that much.

My eyes traveled up to the jacket he was wearing, tight on his biceps, and slightly unzipped. He was the exact opposite of every other coach in the league who wore khakis and polos. Most head coaches were in their sixties, but Coach Peyton made NFL history when the Jets took a chance on him a few years ago.

Seemed to have paid off well.

The thirty-second timeout went by too fast, and before I knew it, Coach Peyton was turning from his team and facing me. My eyes shot up from his ass to his face, and I felt the heat forming on my skin from being busted.

His lips quirked up a little, no doubt feeling empowered by catching me ogling, but I quickly recovered and honed back in on the game. The rest of the game went smoothly, and even when Coach Peyton came up to stand beside me, I wasn't fazed.

We seemed to find a normal work mode that I hoped would carry into the rest of the season, and I thanked myself for putting him in his place early. That was the only thing that had changed, and I knew it must have told him that I wasn't one to fuck with.

When the game ended, I happily shook hands with my fellow

referees and made my way down the tunnel to my locker room. Things were looking up, and with the team leaving for an away game the following weekend, that gave me two more weeks to soak it in before the next risk to my sanity emerged.

I slammed the door to my room, forgetting the lock. Taking my shirt off, I threw it in my bag to take home to wash, then started the shower. I took my braid out, piling my hair on top of my head to keep it dry while I rinsed my body of sweat. Since I had plans to work out that evening, I was going to save washing my hair for afterward.

I was just beginning to unbutton my pants when the door to my room slammed open and then shut. I looked up, almost wanting to scream at the invasion, but a charging Levi Peyton cut me off.

His hands wrapped around my neck, not enough to hurt, but enough to let me know he was in charge. It was like some power play, a way to exert his dominance after being decimated by my words on the field. And as I suspected, that was the first thing he brought up.

"You need to watch the way you talk to me out there. The cameras are always watching."

I laughed under the pressure of his hand. Even in my bra, with my pants unzipped, I didn't feel weak. I didn't feel scared even when he reached up from my neck to squeeze my cheeks.

His face was close to mine, and he was staring into my eyes, waiting for me to cower to his superiority. He had a lot of nerve, barging into my room, threatening me, and putting his hands on me. We were, after all, in a very scrutinized position, as coach and ref, in the very public eye of the NFL.

"Likewise, *Coach*," I spat at him. "You better watch the way you talk to me as well."

"Or what?"

"Exactly, or what?"

He backed away just slightly, enough to gauge the meaning behind my eyes. But I gave nothing away. You didn't find success in my job–both jobs–by being a coward. Did I want to lose my job before I started? No. Did I want things to get ugly between Levi and me? No.

But I didn't fear any outcome as long as I knew I held my own and kept my dignity intact. I couldn't change what happened in New York, and until last week, I didn't even regret it. I was willing to bet Levi didn't either.

Now, there we were, in a battle of wills, trying to remain focused while keeping the world oblivious to our connection.

"You have a lot of nerve coming in here like this," I whispered. I glanced up to the TV where the post-game show was waiting on Coach Peyton for a post-game interview.

"I have enough to worry about without you being on that field, distracting me."

"Likewise."

"Then let's agree to stay out of each other's way."

"Is that what you are going to do when I make a call you don't agree with?"

He leaned in close and lowered his voice. "I'm going to treat you like every other referee who makes shitty calls."

"So, what should I do?"

"Do what every other ref does. Ignore me."

I laughed because he was serious, but ignoring him seemed impossible. "That will be easier when you don't have your hand around my throat and your dick against my stomach."

Like a light switching on, his brain kicked into what he was doing, and he backed away quickly. Through his joggers, I could see he had gotten hard while being pressed against me, and I wanted to moan at how much I wished I was anyone else in the world so I could feel him again.

He was in too much of his own daze to notice how affected I

was, and I wasn't even sure he knew he had gotten hard while holding me. It took him a solid minute before he shook his head, adjusted his dick, and opened the door to my room. He slammed it shut when he left, and instead of feeling like I won a battle, I walked myself into the shower, pants still on, and sank to the ground.

Something told me that it would always be that way between us because I learned that, without a doubt, what made us angriest was the one thing we couldn't fix, even if we wanted to.

Our undeniable sexual tension.

levi

"AGAIN!" I shouted, hoping the guy I just beat down would get up and go for another round.

"Levi, enough man," my brother shouted from outside the ring. "Poor guy needs a breather."

I backed away, looking at the guy I had never met before. He agreed to spar, but he had no idea he was dealing with a lunatic with so much pent-up energy. I nodded at him that I was done, and he took off out of the ring while I turned and looked at my brother.

Rhys Peyton, my little brother, had come into town to see our first preseason game, and decided I needed a babysitter until I could get myself in check. He was a star soccer player for the Miami Inferno, but had to miss the last few weeks of his season due to injury. Therefore, he had no plans to leave.

And I had no plans on telling him what was really wrong.

"This job is tearing away at you," he suggested. That was true, so I let him keep thinking that was all.

"The pressure never ends. I thought being a player was hard."

He opened the ropes for me, and I climbed out of the ring.

"Even after proving you can win, they still want to bring you down, huh?"

"The world won't be happy until I win without Cam Nichols at quarterback."

"That's just stupid since Cam has repeatedly hyped you for being the reason his game has been on point."

I just shrugged and headed to the locker room to shower and change. My little brother had no idea how many words were said just to be politically correct. Was that what Cam did? I had no idea. I definitely felt like I contributed to the entire team being cohesive and conditioned, but what did I know? I was the idiot who stalked into Charleigh Wright's private locker room, held her by the throat, threatened her, and got hard while doing it. So, I wasn't much for good judgment at that moment.

Once I was showered and changed, I met Rhys in the lobby of the gym and started to suggest dinner, but was stopped by the owner of the gym, Albert Conner.

"Coach? Can I have a word?" Al asked.

I nodded and motioned to my brother to give me one more second before I joined Al in his office. "What's up?"

"I haven't seen you for months, and you come in here like Rambo, going through my guys like a running back against a weak defense. What gives?"

I laughed at Al, and also regretted being away from the gym for so long. I had started working out at the complex because that was where I always was, but being back in the old gym with guys who weren't involved in the NFL was nice.

"Damn, Al, can't a guy get a workout in?"

"Yeah, but damn, kid, you're scaring everyone out of the ring."

"A lot of stress, what can I say?"

"Well, I'm gonna have to outsource your opponents if you don't chill a little. I spoke with my friend Bobby, he might have a few you can spar with, but I'm not sure who's in your weight and age class. They may make you cry, Coach."

I instantly perked up at the idea of someone bigger and younger than me wanting to go head-to-head. Fighting was a rush, and even though I knew I needed to let it go, it was the only thing that kept my mind off Charleigh.

"You bring whoever you need to, Al. I need all the punches I can get to make it through this season."

"Your funeral. When you want it?"

"Next Monday, when I get back to town."

"Okay, but it may need to be at their place, and it's in a rougher neighborhood. No fancy pants penthouses down there."

I rolled my eyes.

Once upon a time, I didn't have a penthouse either. I had a two-bedroom house in downtown Oakland. A hard neighborhood, with a mom who worked her ass off to make sure we didn't end up on the streets after my dad split on us.

Being able to play sports saved our lives. Not just mine and my brother's, but hers as well. We both went to college on sports scholarships, and the day we went pro, we made sure Mom was taken care of. I was the oldest, and the first to see the dollars hit my account, so I bought her a new house in a safer part of town.

By the time Rhys had his first paycheck dropped into his account, he ensured she had everything she could ever want. She still worked and stayed active in the community, though. She even took kids under her wing who needed a safe place to turn.

The bottom line was, I wasn't some pretty boy who was too scared to cross over to the wrong side of the tracks–especially for a good fight.

"Just leave my name out of it, and I'll go wherever," I told Al. I didn't need everyone down there knowing the head coach of the Jets was looking for a fight.

"I'll text you when I know something," Al agreed.

I left his office and nudged my brother, who was looking down at his phone. "Let's go."

We walked the few blocks back to my apartment building near Centennial Park in downtown Atlanta. I bought the entire top-floor penthouse when I signed on to coach the Jets. It wasn't as extravagant and ritzy as some penthouses, but it was secluded and quiet. It gave me a safe place to escape to when the media just wanted to hound me.

I tossed my bag onto the floor, too tired to care where I threw it, and headed into the kitchen while Rhys made his way into the living room. Reaching into the fridge, I grabbed a beer and twisted the top, gulping half of it down without a breath. I could hear him switch on the sports news channel, and cringed when the first thing I heard was my name.

"Do you have to watch that shit?" I yelled around the wall that separated the kitchen from the living room, then took another swig.

"I want to see how the league is doing," he yelled back, meaning Major League Soccer. "Not my fault your ass yelled at the pretty ref and made headlines again."

I almost spewed the beer from my mouth as I left the kitchen and rounded the corner to see what he was looking at. On the screen was a freeze frame of Charleigh waving her arms to mark a first down, and me standing behind her on the sidelines, looking like I would kill her if I had the chance.

"Fuck, they're just searching for a story," I mumbled. That was all they wanted from me, and I was close to giving it to them. Charleigh had a lot of nerve talking to me the way she did on the sidelines, but I would give her credit because the whistle in her mouth made it impossible to read her lips.

The indescribable rage I felt toward her was having the opposite effect I had hoped it would. After our last game, a madman emerged from me, and I blew into her locker room without even thinking of repercussions. Seeing her in her bra didn't stop me either. Hell, I had seen more than that of her before.

A lot more.

Instinct had taken over my body, and holding her against the wall had been mindless. Except for my dick, he seemed to know exactly what we were doing, and who we were with. He seemed to have a mind of his own.

I listened for a minute while the TV announcers droned on about their "insight" into my body language, and frustrations toward Charleigh. Only after they all agreed that I was treating her like I would every other referee did I unclench my fist and lower my tight shoulders. I turned and headed to my room, mumbling about how they didn't know anything.

I was definitely not treating her like every other referee because not once had I slammed one against a wall and gotten hard against their body.

Fuck.

I needed another shower.

charleigh

"YO CHARLEIGH," Bobby called for me as I was getting ready to leave Friday. "I got something for ya."

I lifted my head to give him my attention, but continued the process I had started of shoving my gym clothes into a bag. "What's up?"

"Monday afternoon, my buddy Al needs someone for a spar. Who ya got?"

"Weight class?"

"Two-twenty."

"Age?"

"He said it didn't matter."

I looked around at the nearly empty gym, trying to think of who had been there earlier and who might have wanted a work-out. I had only become a part of the ring because of my brother, but after a while, I became good at getting guys to focus and fight. Two-twenty was too heavy for me to fight, but I was tempted to accept just to have an excuse to hit someone.

"You know Sisco is looking for a fight. Or even Bond. Axton is working with the kids Monday so he's out."

"Yeah, Sisco. It will be good to spar with another gym. I can work with him this weekend to get him ready." Sisco was on parole and loved to hang out at the gym. He was one of Bobby's free customers, just to give him a place to go to stay out of trouble.

"I'll be here Monday to cheer him on."

"I'll need you to call it," Bobby added, pointing at me.

"Of course."

Monday came and I felt refreshed. Not having to be at the stadium and subject to Coach Peyton's wrath was nice. It made me rethink why I ever wanted to be a professional football official in the first place.

Then I remembered I wouldn't be having those issues if I hadn't slept with the one coach I had to have standing behind me every Sunday. I had no way of foreseeing that in my future when I made my career plans.

"Sisco, you ready?" I asked as I watched him practice his punches on a punching bag.

"Hell yeah," he growled. "Where's this chump?"

I looked around and saw Bobby and his friend Al talking and laughing near the door to the gym. It looked like we were still waiting on whoever wanted their ass beaten by Sisco.

"Take it easy, Big Guy, save some punches for the ring."

Sisco nodded and turned to one of his buddies for some water. I started making my way to Bobby, hoping to find out if the fight was going to happen, or if I'd spent most of the morning hyping Sisco up for no reason.

I was ten feet away when the front doors to the gym opened and the sun beamed in around a tall, muscular figure. Bobby and Al brightened up and shook hands with the guy I assumed was there to spar. Behind him was another guy, almost the same stature, but with the sun gleaming around them, all I could make out were their silhouettes.

Then the door closed, pushing the sun back out into the streets, leaving my eyes in a haste to adjust again. But once they did, I wished I could go back to being oblivious. I wished I'd never seen who was standing in the front talking to Bobby.

Levi Peyton.

I watched the Jets' game on TV the day before and they lost pretty badly during their away game. Coach Peyton was frustrated and kept taking off his headset to run a hand through his hair. He would stand there as the camera zeroed in on him, his hands on his hips and his face a mask of anger.

How was he that same happy guy I met in New York?

The present version of him seemed to be fueled with rage. Or maybe that was just the way he was during football season.

I did take note of the announcer's discussion, though, and how much they were trying to find fault in his every move. Being Levi Peyton didn't seem like a fun job, so I tried to shake off some of his anger toward me. I was merely another level of stress for him.

Which I understood because, in return, it leveled up the stress for me as well.

"Charleigh!" Bobby yelled and motioned for me to join them.

I hesitated for a fraction of a second, but decided that avoiding them would only make things worse.

Levi looked up at me, his eyes widening again, much like they did on the field when he first noticed who I was. He wiped his hand down his face and shook his head as he took two steps backward to the door.

He wanted to run; I could see it written all over him. But to his credit, he stayed put.

"Hi," I smiled, unsure which version of Levi I was getting.

"Charleigh, this is Brett. He and Sisco are gonna go five rounds."

I raised up an eyebrow at him and tilted my head, finding it a little funny that Coach Peyton showed up at Bobby's Gym as "Brett." It also sent a little exhilaration running through me because it was "Brett" that I had been missing. Brett was funny, hot, demanding, dirty, and sexy. Brett said things in my ear no man had ever dared to say before. Brett held my hand as we made our way to his room. Brett pushed me against a wall and fucked me so hard I almost blacked out. Then, Brett did it again. And again.

I had never, and will probably never again, be fucked the way Brett fucked me.

My face started to give my thoughts away, so I turned around and looked back over my shoulder. "This way, *Brett*."

I walked off, hoping he would follow me so I didn't have to look back again. Motioning toward the locker room, I waved him in and told him Sisco was ready to rumble.

He didn't say anything to me, not even a thank you. As I left him and his friend to go into the locker room, I started making my way back to Sisco.

"Charleigh?" Al stopped me, and I smiled. I put my hand out to shake his and gave him my best welcome.

"Yes, sir, nice to meet you."

He looked worried and hesitant, but after he shook my hand and gazed around the room quickly, he leaned in closer to me. "You know who he is, don't you?"

My jaw dropped because he was clearly talking about Coach Peyton and I really didn't want to talk about him at all. But I couldn't deny it. Al obviously saw my face morphing a million different ways earlier.

"Yes," I whispered. It seemed important to Al that we stayed quiet.

"Look, I told him the backward hat wasn't going to fool anyone," Al started, looking off at the ring that sat in the center of the room while he spoke. "But can we keep who he is, and the fact that he is here, between us? The guy works out at my gym and has been going through some things. He just needs to spar. Helps settle him down."

I was still frozen, waiting for Al to keep talking, but when he glanced my way, I realized he was done. What did I say? I didn't want Al to know I was the new NFL official, so fair was fair.

"Yeah, sure. I mean, it's not my business."

"Thank you," Al breathed. "He started back in the gym a couple of weeks ago and has been going through my guys like pinatas at a kid's birthday party. He needs this match up to let out whatever he's going through."

Curiosity got the best of me, and Al seemed like a talker, so I dared to ask, "What's he going through?"

"Fuck, I don't know. He went off to New York for some meetings a few months ago and when he got back, he stopped coming into the gym. I would check in on him, but he seemed good, like whatever his meetings were about were enough to settle him down a little. Levi has been coming to the gym and fighting for a couple of years. It helps him release all that stress."

I nodded because I knew what he meant. It was the same reason I got in the ring sometimes. It was cathartic, punching someone in a safe and monitored environment. There were rules and structure, so all you had to do was follow those rules and let the therapy session take root.

"A couple of weeks ago, he showed up after a game and said he needed to punch something, and has been on a tear since." Al was still talking, still oversharing. But he was speaking almost like a father who cared about Coach Peyton and wanted someone else to know what he had been going through.

"Well, Sisco will make it hard on him," I elbowed Al and

walked off, letting the conversation die. I didn't want to know anything else about Levi Peyton. He needed to remain the asshole coach who griped about my play calls and cussed me out behind my back. Not the guy who showed up to fight it out in the ring. That was the kind of guy I could relate to more than he knew, and I didn't want to relate to him at all.

I was standing near the ring when he came out of the locker room. He was in boxing shorts, a t-shirt, had his gloves on, and his wrists taped up. He met up with Al, who guided him to the other side of the ring.

Not once did he glance my way, but I knew he knew I was watching. He listened as Al put his headgear on for him and hyped him up a little.

It reminded me that I was supposed to be doing that for Sisco, not staring at the opponent. Luckily, Sisco was already in full fight mode and was taking jabs at the air behind me.

"Sisco!" I yelled, getting his attention. I motioned for him to get in the ring, and he climbed under the ropes gracefully. He shook his shoulders out and bounced around while I did what Bobby paid me to do. "Okay, listen up. This one looks like a pretty boy; you may have to go easy on him."

Sisco stopped moving and stared at me. He had never been told to go easy. He probably didn't even understand the words. I chanced a peek up at Coach Peyton and realized he had heard what I said. Then I looked back at Sisco and laughed.

"Just kidding, Big Guy. Have fun and leave some marks."

Sisco never lost. He fought by the rules and was a good opponent. He was a good sportsman as well. But his long, powerful arms were too much for everyone he ever fought. At 28 years old, Sisco was in better shape than anyone else in the gym, no matter their age or how strong they were.

"Let's do this," Bobby shouted, calling for Sisco to leave me in the middle of the ring. I had almost forgotten Bobby asked me to call the fight. As a member of the gym, I helped prep Sisco, but now I had to get into officiating mode.

Holy shit, I thought to myself, realizing that Levi was about to learn that I was once again the official who was standing in his way. I imagined he was going to lose his mind. When Sisco landed a knockout blow, he would blame me for not calling a fair fight.

But I couldn't back out. Having his buddy, Al, in the gym was making it all extra fun for Bobby. That was why he didn't want to call the fight himself. It was like a friendly rivalry for them, and Bobby wanted to be in Sisco's corner, not in the middle of the punches.

"Okay guys," I breathed, making it clear I was the referee. "Come meet in the center."

Levi's eyes narrowed in on me as Al pulled the shirt over his head. My mouth inadvertently started to drool at seeing his bare chest again. Fuck, I once licked that entire chest, and bit his nipples just to tease him.

How am I going to do this?

"Let's have a clean fight," I said once they made their way to the center. "Touch hands and then back to your corners."

They did as I instructed, but I could tell Levi was wary of the fact that I was refereeing. Surely, he could understand by now that officiating was what I did, right?

I motioned for Bond to ring the bell, and in an instant, they were swinging fists and throwing punches.

Meanwhile, I was left in a state of complete shock.

levi

RHYS and I had been running five minutes behind schedule because I spent most of my morning getting yelled at by Richard for the loss the day before. He seemed to take our first loss extremely badly, and used it as a way to threaten me into doing things the way I didn't want to do them. I had worked for him for four years, and each year got worse with his involvement in how I coached the team.

He didn't understand that for even the best teams in the world, winning one hundred percent of the time wasn't sustainable. His ideas and perspectives made me irate.

However, his call did give me fuel to go punch someone. Mix that with seeing Charleigh in the same gym, and my head nearly exploded.

I couldn't get over the odds. Fate was almost fucking with me too hard. Rhys had to snap me out of a daze three times while I got dressed, and put my gloves on. He rambled on, and I barely listened to him talk, but I was sure he was just trying to fill the silent air in the room.

Only after he said how "hot" Charleigh was did I snap back into fight mode. Charleigh may have been a pain in my ass, the stress I didn't need, and made my body do things against its will, but she wasn't his to notice. She was mine.

I knew I could never have her again, and I wasn't even sure I would if I could. But hearing my brother talk about how hot she was made me possessive and manic. The worst part was, I was sure he noticed the shift in me, maybe even said it on purpose to test me.

Thankfully, he didn't call me out on it. He let it stew inside of me until I was practically running from the locker room to fight.

I should have known she would be asked to referee since that was what she did, but it still shocked me again when she started the fight. It crossed my mind that she wouldn't call a fair fight. That fight was her chance to get back at me for every little thing I said to her on the field. For every play I thought she blew, and for barging into her locker room the week before.

When the bell rang, I went right in and started jabbing at Sisco. He was a large man with an ankle monitor on, and I had no doubt he was looking for a fight just as hard as I was. According to Al, Sisco was undefeated in the ring, and everyone expected him to stay that way.

Despite our age difference, Sisco had no idea what was about to happen to him. I wasn't giving my little Apple any room to call a "bad game." Not when she was the reason I started sparring again in the first place.

I made Sisco wear himself down first, making him swing and miss over and over again. By the third round, I knew I needed to swing back, and even though I didn't want to KO anyone in a small gym fight like that, I was about to send Sisco home with a serious headache.

"Round three," Charleigh yelled, and the bell sounded for the round to begin.

I walked slowly to the middle, almost acting as if I was bored. I even chanced a glance at Charleigh, who was eyeing me as I approached. She was wearing the tiniest pair of shorts I had ever seen, a sports bra, and a tank top that dipped so low on the sides that I could see the bare skin of her waist.

I had picked her up by that waist and thrown her legs over my shoulders. I'd licked and nipped at her pussy until she came, making her scream "Brett" so loud that I was sure the people in the other room were going to complain.

If I could go back, I would tell her my name was Levi because for the last three months, I wondered what my real name on her lips would have sounded like.

Focusing back on the fight, I avoided a few more jabs from Sisco before I found my opening. He was tired, wobbling, and although I knew he could still knock me out, he was slowing down too much to land a blow.

As he jabbed his right arm toward my jaw, I blocked him with my left forearm and took my right hand up under his jaw. The contact was hard, and sent Sisco to the mat. He rolled side to side as everyone encouraged him to get up, but when it was apparent that he was too dazed to continue, Charleigh called the fight.

Al and Rhys cheered as I leaned down to help Sisco up. He had sat up and was shaking the metaphorical birds away as they swirled around his head.

"Good fight, man," I offered my hand, and he took it, bro-hugging me and then bowing from the ring. It was tradition to have the winner's arm raised, even in a small gym fight, but the one who would raise it was Charleigh and I wasn't letting her touch me in front of so many people. The chances of my dick forgetting the memo of not being able to touch her was high–just like in her locker room.

Instead, I nodded toward Bobby and glanced at Charleigh before sliding under the rope and heading to the locker room.

"Give me a minute," I told Rhys, not wanting to be followed. I needed to decompress and the only way I knew to do that was to be alone.

"I gotta book a charter flight, anyway. Meet you outside."

I nodded, acknowledging he had to get back to Miami for a few days to see his doctors. I was content knowing he would be distracted doing that for a bit and turned toward the locker rooms.

The locker room at Bobby's gym had a penurious vibe, but considering it was in a low-income area of Atlanta, I wasn't sure what I expected. It didn't bother me, but I wondered if it would ever see the upgrades it needed, or if it would just fall down one day.

I sat alone in there. No one else seemed to need to use the facility so I decided on a shower since it looked like they had laid a fresh towel out just for me.

Using my teeth, I started ripping away the tape that Rhys had wound around my wrists and gloves. It was hard to do without hands, but I didn't ask for help since I was still basking in solitude.

Or so I thought.

"Let me do it," Charleigh's voice startled me. I wasn't sure when she came in, or why she was even there, but I nodded at her offering.

She walked closer to me and grabbed my wrist, unraveling the tape little by little. We stayed quiet, but I watched her, looking at her face for any signs as to what would lead her into the men's locker room with me. Her eyes stayed focused on my wrist, but she could read my questioning stare without having to look at me.

"Fair is fair," she shrugged, holding her hand out for my other wrist. With the first hand free, I could have easily taken over the process, but I gave her my arm and let her do it. "You burst into my locker room; I'm busting into yours."

I smirked, seeing her logic as almost cute. "Are you going to push me against a wall?"

She didn't answer; just smiled and kept working on my second wrist. Once I was free, she pulled the gloves off my hands and backed away from me a few feet. "I'll return that favor some other way."

"Like demeaning my dick on the sidelines?"

"You deserved that."

"A man never deserves to have his dick talked down to like that."

"And a woman never deserves to be pushed against a wall while she is trying to undress."

I stood up, towering over her and taking a step closer. "You didn't mind in New York."

"Yeah, well," she crossed her arms over her chest and rolled her eyes, "New York was headed toward a happy ending. You were just bullying me last week."

I stayed quiet and squinted my eyes at her. Truthfully, I *was* bullying her. She pissed me off just by being there, and being so untouchable. She added more stress to my job by just being there. I had been losing control more and more since she turned around to face me at that first game.

"What are you doing here, at the gym?" I asked, annoyed that she was invading yet another part of my life. My tone spoke of my discontent, and she picked up on it.

"I've worked here for years. This place is a second home to me, so it kinda feels like I should be asking *you* that?"

I didn't owe her any explanations. She saw by my fight with Sisco that it wasn't my first time. No one in my football life knew I boxed, though, and I started to ask her to keep it to herself.

"See ya next Sunday, *Brett*," she turned before I could say anything else, not forcing me to explain. I didn't bother asking her to keep quiet about my extracurricular activities either.

Boxing wasn't against the rules, but Richard frowned upon anything that could cause harm to players and coaches. Some guys even had it in their contracts that they weren't allowed to take risks, such as skydiving, or driving motorcycles. I didn't, but the owner of the Jets would lose his shit if he knew I took hits to the head once a week.

He would also use it as an excuse to fire me from my contract.

Charleigh left, but I came close to pulling her into my lap while she was there. It was hard to see her outside of the stadium and remember that we had to be enemies. The word enemies may have been dramatic, but that was how it felt. We had to stay angry, even if it didn't make sense. It was the only way we could keep our jobs.

The league didn't excuse misunderstandings. They wouldn't care that we had no idea who each other was at the time. Once we'd figured it out, that would have been the best time to fess up. But weeks had passed and we were stuck with our secrets.

charleigh

I HAD WALKED in that locker room ready to yell and scream, give him everything he gave me when he invaded my personal space. But then I saw him sitting there, his shoulders slumped, and tearing at his tape with his teeth.

Call me weak, but I couldn't be as cold to him as he was with me, especially when we were not on the field. As a fighter, I saw him differently, punching away his demons and stress. I was also in shock that he beat Sisco. No one had ever done that, and even though their sizes were comparable, Levi seemed softer by default.

Pampered.

When I met him in New York, he was wearing a tailored suit and tie. Something with an expensive name and high-end threads. I pictured him getting facials and having someone drive him everywhere.

Even when I pieced together that he was a football coach, I couldn't separate him from the well-dressed, put-together "Brett" I met before. Now, I saw him a little differently. I still wanted to rip his face off for being such a jerk, but I was curious. I wanted to know what had led him to the ring. Why would he risk his pretty face for a match?

I mulled on that all week, and even as I watched his interviews on TV, I couldn't piece the two sides of him together. He obviously used "Brett" as his alias when he didn't want anyone to know who he was.

The only thing that got under my skin now was his vehemence toward me. Couldn't we agree to stay quiet and civil? Who cared if I was the referee? I still intended on calling a fair game.

When I walked into the stadium for the final preseason game that following Sunday, that was the mindset I had, to be civil and call a good game. After being around each other in the gym, surely, we had come to a modicum of understanding.

"Hey Ms. Wright," Martin smiled and waved as I walked onto the field. I gathered with my fellow officiating team and chatted about the game. Same stuff we always talked about—who to keep an eye on, what the teams were known for, and at what level we would let them "play it out."

Not every penalty deserved a flag. Sometimes, we had to be objective and not throw the flag, and that was something we were going to try to do for that last preseason game. It made me nervous, though. Despite the uniforms we wore, calls were never black and white. But being told to make an effort to "no-call" was making me jittery. Any progress I made with Coach Peyton last Monday was going to go up in flames the second I didn't call pass interference against the other team when they tested one of his precious tight ends.

I glanced at the sideline, where Coach Peyton watched his team warm up. He had his legs spread, his arms crossed, and a clipboard dangling from one hand. His eyes were darting from his quarterback to his wide receivers, then back to his defense. How he kept track of everyone was impressive.

The officials around me got off-topic, and talked about their wives, kids, and grandkids. I had none of that, so I was lost inside my own head, watching Coach Peyton, and trying once again to combine him with "Brett".

His face looked stressed–even more than usual–like whatever was going on inside his head was becoming harder to mask within his features. It couldn't just be me, could it? Surely his stress was coming from somewhere deeper than the line judge he once fucked seven ways to Sunday.

I looked up to the stands to try and avoid looking at him. The fans were filling in as we were only thirty minutes from the start of the game. It never ceased to amaze me how much football fans craved the live games. Didn't matter at all that it was preseason. A packed house and aggressive fandom would be happening right down to the last tick of the clock.

Then I read the scrolling on the signs as they made their way around the stadium, taking time to read each and every promotion the team had. I looked at my nails to check for dirt. I checked my shoes to make sure they matched. Anything to keep me from looking back to Coach Peyton.

When I looked at the team, taking note that Tyson Black wasn't even on the field, that led me right back to wondering about Coach Peyton's stress being more than just me. I inadvertently took my eyes back to him, hoping for a quick glimpse, but instead of being able to look away with no one knowing, I found myself wrapped up in the opposing stare of his gorgeous eyes.

I couldn't turn away. It was like we had caught each other and were now at war to see who would look away first. Something about him made me not want ever to lose, so I tilted my head and kept my eyes on his. He narrowed his eyes a little, taunting me back, but I knew I would win that fight. He had a team to coach, and I had nothing to do for twenty-five more minutes.

He licked his lips, but it didn't feel as though it was on

purpose. It was a reflex, and my responding reflex was to moan under my breath. The sound I made was quiet, but it snapped me out of my daze. I couldn't moan for that man, especially not there on the field.

I averted my eyes, hoping no one heard me, while also losing the fight. I hated myself instantly, but when I looked back to Coach Peyton, I saw no look of triumph. He was still looking at me like he was trying to figure something out that I didn't understand.

Then, with a small jerk of his head, he turned and walked from the field. The team followed him, taking their fifteen-minute break before the game started, and the officials remained on the field. But I needed my own minute, something to cool me down before I stood so close to Coach Peyton on the sideline for three hours.

"I'll be right back," I nodded toward the corridor. "Gonna change my socks really quick."

The looks of concern and confusion from my co-officials were warranted. Who the hell needed to change their socks? It was just the only thing I could think of that wouldn't be noticeable when I returned. Telling them I was considering pinching my nipples to ease the pain of them hardening while I stared at Levi Peyton didn't seem like a good idea.

I started jogging so I had more time in my locker room, even considering how long it would take to bring myself to an orgasm just to take the edge off. When I got in the room, I leaned against the door and squeezed my eyes shut, willing my body not to want his.

The TV in my small locker room was on the broadcast and I looked up to see a commercial about orphaned dogs. I tried hard to let myself cry for those dogs. I imagined what it must be like for them, and how I wished I could save them all.

But even that didn't work. Once the commercial ended, I was

right back in my head about my stare-off with Coach Peyton. I walked to the sink and splashed some water on my face, then headed back to the door.

I yanked it open with frustration and made the two steps around the corner to the main walkway. Just as I stepped out, I was side by side with him, like some cruel twist of karma for sleeping with him in the first place.

He was leading his team out and there were cameras all around. It was being broadcast onto the big screens in the stadium and I knew I had to get as far away from that as possible.

"Sorry," I muttered to no one, and sped up to get past the cameras. I took one last glance backward, like the masochist I was, and saw Coach Peyton watching me walk away. He swallowed so hard I could see his Adam's apple move, and then he bit his lip.

I turned back and ran, because even though I wasn't convinced he was doing it on purpose, it started to feel methodical on his part. A different way to win the war. I needed distance, and I needed it quickly.

Running from the corridor, I caught up to my officiating team and made a quick joke about how much better my socks felt. Then we looked up to watch the teams being announced and led out onto the field.

Fireworks were blasting, music was playing, and the fans were so loud I barely heard Martin telling us to have a good game. I shook the hands of each of my co-workers and made my way to the home team's sideline, just as Coach Peyton did.

With the game starting and everyone looking his way, he paid me less attention, and I was beyond thankful. He took his headset and settled it on his ears, and I pulled my smaller one out and settled the bud into my right ear.

We gave each other a practiced nod, something everyone else would expect between two professionals. But somehow, the air around us had changed. Being close to him had been hard from the start, but now that I had the image of him sending Sisco to the mat in my head, I was jittery and apprehensive.

I kept wondering if he was as fucked up as I was. While I settled in my position to call the game, and he settled into coach, I wondered if he was watching me from behind. Thank the football Gods that the coach had to stay behind the line judge because there was not a doubt in my mind I wouldn't survive the game if he was in my view.

The game started, and to my relief, I was able to forget about the man behind me and do my job. There had also been no close calls in the first half, so I had no need to throw my flag, which was the best way to keep Coach Peyton out of my hair.

It wasn't until the game neared the end that sparks started to fly again, and not the good kind. Sparks like ammo and gunpowder, old outlets, and lightning near telephone poles. Just as I predicted, the defense for the opposing team tangled up with one of the Jets' tight ends, Lawrence Anders, and even though I could have thrown the flag for a penalty, it was a "let them play" situation and Coach Peyton was letting me hear all about it.

"We are leaving here after this game and going straight to the Ophthalmologist. I swear to God you cannot see anything."

"Calm down Coach. We're letting them play it out." I said the words Martin told me to say, but all they did was drive Coach Peyton crazier.

"You think I give a shit? You think this is a fucking game?"

I turned around, amusement all over my face. "Really, Coach? A game? That's exactly what this is."

"No, it's my job, and you making calls like that doesn't come down on you. They come down on me."

"Hey, hey, hey..." the assistant, who I knew was named Dave, was pulling at Levi, trying to lead him away. "Calm down."

"I'm not calming down. Is this how it will be all season,

Apple? Gonna be fucking everything up when you spend more time looking at the players, and not the play?" I flinched at his use of my one-night stand name, but everyone else thought it was an insult. It wasn't. Insinuating I was ogling the players was the insult. Another jab at me for not being good enough for the job based on my gender.

I put my hands on my waist and faced him, my eyes beading and my whistle in my mouth. The assistant coach was trying so hard to pull Coach Peyton away that it was almost comical.

How was it that he looked even better when he was in a fit of rage? Rage directed at me? It was like I had a defective attraction meter, and instead of finding a nice, calm, and civilized man to lust after, my body chose the crazy coach.

While he was still yelling, I grabbed my flag from my waist-band and brought it up into my hand. Then, like the petty woman I felt like being, I gently tossed it at his feet and blew my whistle.

I waved my arms, indicating I had called another penalty, and Coach Peyton stood as still as a statue as I smirked behind my whistle. Then I turned to Martin, who was approaching me for the penalty call, and I shouted to him so everyone could hear.

"Personal Foul on the coach, abusive language toward an official."

Martin nodded and made the announcement, moving the Jets fifteen yards back and out of field goal range. I turned back to get to my spot on the line, but Coach Peyton was still not moving.

His arms were crossed, his headset was tossed to the ground, and he was eyeing me like he was dead set on killing me after the game.

When I got closer, I turned around in front of him and blew my whistle again to signal I was ready to resume. Only then did he come up close to me. He didn't say anything, not even to his team. But it was awkward as the game ensued.

Finally, I couldn't take it. I looked toward him, tilted my head a little, and said, "Should have stopped at the eye doctor comment. That was actually a good one."

levi

I STEWED beside Charleigh as the Jets lost the game, not being able to overcome the fifteen-yard penalty flag that she threw at me.

Fuck her.

The guys in my headset who coached from the booth told me she made a good call. They watched the replay over and over again and said it was right. But that didn't matter when, ultimately, she threw the flag at my feet in an obvious act of spite. The cameras and the world probably wouldn't have even caught the difference, but I did. I knew enough about Charleigh Wright to know when she tilted her head a little, she was raging inside.

Join the party, Apple.

As I ran to the center of the field to shake hands with the opposing head coach, I saw Charleigh being pulled off to the side by a few people. No one of importance, probably just someone wanting to kiss her ass, as she apparently made history in the NFL. But it was just enough of a distraction to keep her on the field as long as I was.

By the time I started jogging back to the corridor, she was doing the same along the side of the wall where the fans booed her for the penalties. I laughed a little to myself and slowed down to watch the show, wanting to revel in her affliction from the fans.

"You suck, you stupid cunt!"

"Bitch needs to get off the field."

"You better watch your back, LJ."

I cringed a little, not liking how they talked to her. Sure, I had no room to talk since I had threatened her at every turn, but that was *my* job, not theirs. She kept her head lowered and had almost made it to the entrance to the corridor when a fan threw a beer can at her. On instinct, I ran a few feet to get to her and wrapped an arm around her back, guiding her away from the crowd.

I motioned to security as I held on tight to Charleigh, my arm moving up over her shoulder and pressing her face into my neck to protect her from any more flying objects. I forced her to walk faster, the crowd getting even crazier as they realized I was helping the referee escape their wrath.

"Traitor!"

"You need to be fired!"

"Whose side are you on, Coach?"

I ignored them, and by the time we cleared the area, security was taking over. We walked farther into the corridor, but for some reason, I didn't want to let her go until we were in her locker room. She wasn't fighting me either.

She reeked of stale beer, and her hat was nowhere to be found, lost in the mess we had left behind. She didn't seem upset, just anxious to get to her room.

Once we were there, I mustered enough strength to push her away, not wanting her to think I cared more than I did, because I didn't.

"Ahhhh," she yelled as she righted herself against the door to her room. "Should I say thanks?"

We were around a small corner, out of the eyes of anyone

walking by, so I got closer to her and leaned in. "Yeah, you owe me one."

"I don't owe you shit," she laughed. "You didn't have to do that; I would have made it without you."

"Not without a few more beers to the head."

"I like beer," she sneered while simultaneously making a joke.

"I didn't like how they were talking to you," I confessed without meaning to. So, to make sure I was coming across correctly, I added, "No one talks to you that way but me. If you're a bitch, I'll tell you. If you're a cunt, I'll let you know. But that is not their place. It's mine!"

I slapped the door above her head on the last word, then turned and stomped off. Some part of me felt like a kid throwing a tantrum. None of it made sense to anyone but me, and if someone forced my hand, I wouldn't be able to explain myself.

Instead of heading to my office, I went straight to the post-game press conference, where I knew I was about to field questions about everything from Ty being absent to the penalty I got on the sideline. Even helping the ref off the field. I didn't know what I was going to say about any of it, but the interview was part of my job, and I hoped I would come up with something.

After taking the podium, I wasted no time pointing to reporters who had their hands raised. I didn't need to speak first. I needed to get the hell out of there.

"Coach? Where is Tyson Black?"

"He is taking care of some personal business and will be back soon."

"Coach? What did you say to get the flag thrown at you in the last minute of the game?"

"Wow," I laughed with a guise I was scared they could see through. "Straight for the jugular. I just didn't agree with the call and told the ref I didn't, and she threw the flag."

"Do you feel it was warranted?"

"Do we ever?"

"That wasn't the question, Coach."

I tapped the side of the podium and looked around, thinking quickly about what I wanted to say. "We say a lot of things in the heat of the moment. I will have to go back and review the tape, check out the play, try to remember what I said, and make corrections accordingly so that something like that doesn't cost us in the regular season."

He was getting ready to ask about me helping her off the field. I could see it in his eyes. But everything I had just said summed up the game, and that was all I wanted to say, so instead of waiting for any more questions, I left the stage and walked straight to my office.

Like I normally did, I waited for everyone to leave so I didn't have to face the world. Then I got in my car and called Rhys, thankful he had made it back from Miami already.

"Meet me at the gym. I need something to hit."

"What the fuck, man?" he said, although I wasn't sure what he meant. The gym, the game, the referee?

"Just get over there. I feel like I'm going to explode."

"You may need a therapist. I'm seriously starting to worry about you."

"You have no idea how much pressure I'm under. I don't need a therapist; I need an outlet."

His laugh was gruff, and I could envision him rolling his eyes. "Sex is way less damaging to your face."

It was my turn to roll my eyes. I just wished he could see me. I tried that with the chick at the bar–but it didn't work. If I was being honest, boxing wasn't even helping. Made even worse when I realized Charleigh was a part of that as well.

"Seriously," Rhys laughed again. "You need to get laid."

"Shut the fuck up and meet me at the gym," I laughed so he

knew I was joking and not that unhinged. "You can be my punching bag today."

"Oh joy," he groaned. But I knew he would be there. He knew I needed it and even though Rhys wasn't much of a people pleaser, he would do anything for his big brother.

charleigh

"I CANNOT BELIEVE you threw that flag at his feet," my mom said, laughing as we laced beads onto a string in the middle of her living room. Jesse was there on the couch, watching us, and wanted the TV turned onto the sports channel.

Naturally, my flag was the talk of the town. No one realized how personal that flag was when I threw it, thank God, but they all knew it cost the Jets the game. Everyone wanted to know what Coach Peyton had said to earn it, and not one person around that conversation was talking.

It was funny seeing them try to read his lips, though. *"Gonna be a fucking chicken wing cup when you lend four limes cooking the layers and blot the whey."*

"That is not what he said, was it?" My mom looked up from what she was doing to look at me, but I was busy wondering how the lip readers got it *that* wrong.

"No," I finally laughed. "I don't remember exactly what he said, but it was bad enough I threw the flag." I wanted to spare her the details for some reason. If I told her what he said, she would hate him forever, and for some reason, that didn't sit well with me.

"Well don't do it again," Jesse complained. "The Jets need to win the Super Bowl."

"They've won, like, fifty of them. Isn't that enough?"

"Nooooo," Jesse sat up and crossed his legs. "There are talks of canning the coach if they don't win again."

"Why would they do that?"

"Money," he said matter-of-factly. "The coaches and players love to play, but the owners love money. Winning Super Bowls is the only way Coach Peyton can keep a job. He has to win to pay for his contract."

"That's…" I trailed off, not wanting to call it stupid in front of Jesse. He was a whiz when it came to sports and didn't like when I called anything pertaining to his facts, stupid. Also, Jesse was rarely wrong. He studied everything he was interested in with a deep passion. He was one of the smartest people I had ever met.

"He is under a lot of pressure this season," Jesse continued. "And then with what happened with Tyson Black, I bet it's worse. I want him to stay, he seems nice when he's not yelling. But I don't know of a football coach that doesn't yell."

True.

"What happened to Black?" If anyone knew, it was Jesse.

"Coach Peyton said it was personal. I don't think we will know without reading a book about it."

I nodded, realizing Jesse didn't know any more than I did.

"I'm just going to keep calling the plays as I see them, Jesse," I finally said. "If he wants to win and keep his job, then he can learn not to be a dick."

"Eww," Jesse said, covering his ears like a child.

"He's a good coach," I redirected, just to ease Jesse's sensitive and innocent ears. "He'll find a way to make it work for the team. Maybe he's stressed, but I'm sure he has a nice, healthy coping mechanism."

Like boxing.

I walked into the gym that next Friday, hoping I had a chance to fight my own demons in the ring. That was something I could relate to where Levi Peyton was concerned—we both liked to fight. It was cathartic and soothing in a way that made most people cringe.

I had never been soft, though. You couldn't be when you grew up having to fight for everything you wanted. I was more of a tomboy growing up, and because I wasn't cheery and dainty, I took a lot of shit. But I refused to be someone I wasn't, so I found ways to let out my frustrations. I almost quit when I realized guys didn't like women with a harder punch than them, but I had started taking Jesse with me, and together, it became a full-time passion.

I didn't wear my first dress and heels until I was thirty years old. I thought I would feel like a weak and fussy damsel in distress, but I felt the opposite. I felt like a badass bitch. One that hit heavy bags all day and dressed to kill at night. It was the first time in my life I felt like I knew who I was and what I wanted to do when I grew up.

Plus, I also learned that any man threatened by me was too weak to handle me anyway. Maybe that was why I was so drawn to Levi. He had no qualms about using his size and strength against my own.

I had already been working as a referee, but it was when I turned thirty that I decided to reach for the NFL. I expected to be much older than thirty-five when I reached that goal, but there I was, refereeing pro games.

After a long day, I finally pulled my gloves on and made my

way to the punching bag. No one was around to spar with, but it made for a nice and quiet match against myself. Bobby's was always quiet on Friday nights, so when I needed time to swing punches, that was the night I chose to be there. Conveniently enough, it was also the last chance I had before Sunday games. I tried to make it a ritual during the season to keep my head screwed on tight and focused on the game.

Sunday was a home game for the Jets, so I knew where I would be, and how it would go down. But the Sunday after that, the season's second game, was my first away game, and I was nervous.

I would fly by myself on a commercial flight, and it would be up to me to get to where I needed to be. Not that I wasn't a grown ass woman and couldn't handle it, but the last time I flew to another city alone, I ended up in bed with Coach Peyton.

At least I knew that wouldn't happen again. I wouldn't be in bed with anyone, actually. Because since that night in New York, I had been broken. Levi "Brett" Peyton ruined me. I couldn't even get myself to a climax without thinking of him.

That thought made me pound the bag harder, grunting and screaming. The few people left in the gym didn't bother looking my way. They let me battle it out. Sweat was dripping down my forehead, my shoulders were starting to ache, and I knew I only had five more punches left in me.

One punch for the fact that I had a one-night stand and he showed back up in my life like a devil leaving hell.

Another punch for the fact that I couldn't stop picturing him between my thighs.

A third punch for how disrespectful he was to me on the field.

Number four was for how much I had come to hate him since getting to know him more.

Finally, I reared back and gave it all the strength I had left, one last punch for the night. That one was for the fact that, given the chance, I would fuck him again with no hesitations about what was right or wrong, or how much I hated him.

And for that, I hated myself.

levi

IT WAS the opening game of the regular season, and I had already spent all morning in a meeting with Richard so he could tell me all the things I had done wrong that season.

For starters, I had a black eye. The last-minute fight that Al set up for me on Friday ended up being tougher than I thought. I shouldn't have accepted the bout, but taking the edge off before the big game on Sunday seemed like a good idea at the time.

Now, I was convinced it was a waste. No amount of hitting someone was going to calm my nerves after being told fourteen times in one hour that I was on the chopping block. That if I didn't start bending where he told me to bend, I would be in deep waters. He even pointed to the black eye, asking what happened, and I dug a deeper grave by lying about a door hitting me.

His face said he knew I was lying, and instead of owning up to being in a boxing match with someone forty pounds heavier than me, I just kept the lies coming. *"The door was big. Bulky. I didn't expect it to open. Then 'whack' right in the eye."*

If he hadn't been more worried about how well I coached that first game, he probably would have sent me home just for being a sketchy dick. I probably wouldn't have blamed him at that point.

If I was willing to lie about something so small, what else would I lie about?

When the meeting adjourned, I was able to run to my office and prepare for the game. The players filed in from the hotel across the street where we stayed the night before and were getting ready to take the field for warmups. Including Ty, who had decided to play again after settling his own drama.

Everything had been so consuming that I had almost forgotten about Charleigh. Then she popped out of the alcove to her locker room and started walking ahead of me toward the field. She didn't see me, so the sway of her ass in the straight black pants they forced her to wear wasn't for me. It was just her natural sway and allure. Something so plain shouldn't have been so arousing.

Those pants were made for men, but somehow, she made me lose focus every game she walked back and forth in front of me. Down the line, following the ball and the plays, as I remembered everything under those pants and how her ass felt in my hands.

"Fuck!" I yelled too loud. Everyone that had been walking to the field, including Charleigh, turned to look at me. I held my clipboard in front of my dick, the one that had a mind of its own and hardened without my consent. "Sorry, forgot some papers."

Another lame lie, one that everyone was sure to see right through. I turned and went back to my office, willing myself to get my head back in the game. For good measure, I threw my clipboard into the floor and chalked it up to practicing how I was going to argue her calls later.

When I finally had my shit together, I jogged back to the field and did everything I could not to look her way. No more staring competitions, no more games of chicken. She would win. I had no doubt she was having the same problems I was, getting aroused because of what we had shared in New York. Only her arousal wasn't as apparent as mine and she could hide it while I just walked around like a piece of gym equipment—hard enough to do pull-ups on.

Thankfully, avoiding her was working and I played that hand for all it was worth. She did her job, and I did mine, neither of us causing the other any unwanted issues or drama. But just like in every other game, right before the end of the half, or right before the end of the game, when things were on the line, she fucked up.

The whistle blew as her flag flew, calling our defense for pass interference. Last week, they "let them play," and now she calls it? It had to have been because it was against us. It had to be because she hated me and knew the way to make me suffer the most.

In true Levi Peyton fashion, I threw my headset and clipboard while Dave tried to hold me back with force. "So now you call it?"

She never looked my way, choosing to continue ignoring me as I went on and on about how blind she was–my go-to insult. I didn't even know what I was saying, or what words were coming out of my mouth. The next play happened, and I didn't even have my headset back on. I didn't know what was being called, nor did I care.

I crossed my arms, widened my legs, and stood as still as possible, waiting for the half to end so I could get the hell out of her damn snare.

"Coach," Dave said in my ear, "Replay said it was a good call."

I narrowed my eyes but never looked at him. I was past caring that it was a good call. It still felt personal. In my head, I knew that sounded asinine, but in my pants, it made sense. My dick was offended.

When the whistle finally blew for halftime, I let my team jog ahead of me and I lingered on the field. I wanted to be last, I wanted to walk in close enough to Charleigh so I could lean into her again and leave her in a wake of threats that would make her think twice the next time she pulled the flag from her belt.

Was that right? No.

Was I insane? Possibly.

I started to jog behind her, keeping a little distance until we were in the corridor and away from cameras. After helping her from the field the week before, I knew I needed to be careful so rumors didn't start flying.

I was all set to close the distance just as she was stopped by Richard. He leaned in, too fucking close to her ear, said something quickly, and then walked away.

Charleigh remained frozen, his words clearly rattling her. Richard hadn't seen me, but I was tempted to follow him and demand he tell me what was said. Instead, I followed Charleigh once she started moving again.

Looking at my watch, I knew I had thirteen minutes until the game started back up and instead of spending it with my team, like I should have been, I was going to spend it with her. I wanted to know what Richard said. I still wanted to give her my own warning and settle my unreasonable animosity so that I could have a good season moving forward.

Unfortunately, none of that happened.

charleigh

MR. ELDER'S words chilled me, causing me to freeze for an abnormal amount of time. Up until that moment, Richard Elder had been nothing but nice to me. He was so accommodating and supportive, excited the Jets had the means to host me as part of the officiating crew.

Once he was long gone, I was able to keep walking to my locker room. I needed what time was left to regain my composure. I knew I had that last call right. The defensive guy for the Jets had his arms around the receiver's waist before the ball was even thrown. Had I not made that call, I would have been back on the sports channel being ripped apart for a "no call.'

I didn't mind that part of the job. I didn't mind getting it wrong or right. But the stress seemed to be mounting by the second. I was on the verge of hyperventilating, pacing my room, and worrying about what the fuck I had gotten myself into.

After taking a sip of water and turning back toward the door, Coach Peyton came again barreling into my room. That time, instead of pushing me into the wall, he leaned against the closed door and crossed his arms.

"What the fuck was that about?" he asked with his voice deep and menacing.

"You know as well as I do your guy had the wide receiver wrapped up too early."

"Not that!" he yelled. "What did Richard say to you?"

I leaned back and looked at him like he had three heads. I had a hard time believing that he didn't know what his boss said to me. That he wasn't the one that told Mr. Elder what to say, making this fight between us lopsided. "You know damn well what he said!"

"If I knew," he gritted out, "I wouldn't have asked."

"I'm not going to be bullied, *Brett*. I know after you realized you slept with the new ref you had an opportunity to strong-arm me, but you can't. I would rather tell the world about New York than be forced to call an unfair game."

Now he was looking at me as if I had slapped him. Somewhere deep in my gut, I knew he had no idea what I was talking about. He looked up to the TV, then down to my couch. I could see the wheels in his head spinning, and he was only making me more and more nervous.

"Please leave," I croaked, my voice breaking as I strained to keep my composure.

"You need to calm down, you're too fucked up to go back out there and make good calls."

"That call I made was good!" I repeated.

"You're right, it was. And the calls you make in the second half will be even better."

"I'm sick of the threats, Levi. You're not going to control me. I'm not your puppet—" Before I could finish, I was against the wall, his mouth on mine and his arms lifting me higher. He wrapped my legs around his waist and pushed into my core, his cock so hard I moaned from the pain.

"Calm the fuck down," he repeated. "All eyes are going to be on you, and you have to be cool." His words were spoken against my mouth, and then he moved his lips to my neck. He bit and sucked, just enough to give me pleasure but not enough to leave any marks.

"What—?" I wanted to ask what the fuck he was doing. But I was in so much need for him that I couldn't find the words—or the will to care.

"I know how to calm you down. I know all the right spots, *Apple*." He used my fake New York name to remind me how right he was. "For both our sakes, let me in, and let's make it all go away."

I didn't know how fucking him was going to make it all go away. It seemed like it would only cause us more drama, stress, and animosity. But what did I have to lose? The fight was no longer fair, and I was tired of not feeling any relief or pleasure.

He felt the moment I gave in, my body succumbing to his.

"We have to make this quick, baby. We have to get back on the field in seven minutes. So, I'm going to need you to turn around and lower your pants to your knees. Just like against the window in New York. Remember how quickly we came?"

I nodded, then pushed him off of me, only to do as he said and take my pants down. I remembered exactly how fast we came that first time. We had barely made it inside the room before I turned and placed my palms on the glass.

Just like that night, I tilted my ass into the air. I looked back over my shoulder as he brought the elastic waistband of his joggers below his hard cock and lined himself up with me.

My knees began to shake, so he held my ass cheeks tight to steady me. "Still on the pill? Still clean?" We used a condom before, but we both swapped details of our sexual history as we toyed with each other at the bar.

On my nod, he thrust into me, making us both moan at how well we fit. It was like being in New York all over again. I knew that night that he was a one-night stand. But I also knew that no one had ever fit me the way he had. That was why I could never climax without him. My body wanted *him*.

After months of pent-up tension, not only from not having a release but from the fights Levi and I constantly had, I almost came immediately. Levi was not a boy; he was a man. He knew exactly what to do, how to do it, and had no hold-ups with being as dirty as he had to be to get the job done.

"Fuck, your pussy is perfect." He started moving in and out of me, his hands holding my hips tight like handles. "So fucking wet."

I couldn't respond, my moan was all I could give him. I knew I was making a mistake, but I couldn't feel the regret seep in. I needed it; he needed it. Maybe it was exactly what we needed to move forward. One final fuck and we could let the tension melt away. I knew there was a chance this was all part of their plans to seduce me and control me, but I was at peace knowing I wouldn't let it work.

In fact, I was using him as much as he was using me. Because if I went down, he was going down with me.

"Thumb your clit, Charleigh." His use of my name was magic. Not Apple or Ms. Wright. Charleigh. I wanted him to say it again and again.

I took his direction and reached down to touch myself. Right as my hand felt my clit, his right hand came down on my ass, spanking me hard enough to leave a mark.

"When I see this ass walking down the line in front of me, calling the downs, and throwing those fucking yellow flags, I will know it was mine. I will know you have my handprint on your skin and how dirty we got during halftime."

Another smack landed in the same spot, causing my hand to slip from my clit and back toward his balls as they slapped me from his force. The small touch made his chest rumble and his arms started to shake. I knew he was close, so I let myself go, not even ashamed of how quickly he could make my body submit.

It felt like euphoria. Months and months of pent-up anger and anxiety were released in a way that boxing never could help with. I felt dizzy, but focused, anxious but relieved. I was so confused but I didn't have any regrets. I expected them to come, but they never did.

Levi came with me, grunting his own incoherent words. Then he pulled out of me quickly and pulled my panties up, trapping our combined cum inside. "I'm also gonna know you are walking around out there with my cum in your panties," he said into my ear from behind me.

He pulled my black uniform pants up and as I buckled them, he righted himself. I turned and saw him trying to tuck his cock in a way that would hide it. The giggle that rose up in my throat was hard to suppress, and the eye he cocked at me told me he heard.

Turning toward the door, he flung it open and looked back at me with a stern look on his face. "Make better calls, Charleigh."

"And if I don't?"

He smiled and started closing the door, but I heard him say, "You will," before it slammed shut.

I looked at my watch and had no time actually to clean up, so I really was about to walk onto the field with his cum in my pants. Rolling my eyes at myself, I grabbed a bottle of water and started walking back into the corridor toward the field.

Behind me, I could sense Levi walking with his team like he had just been hanging in the corridor the whole time, no big deal. I wondered if he was already looking at my ass and picturing his handprint.

Just so that I wasn't the only one with their head spinning, I placed my right hand in my back pocket, right over the spot his hand reddened. I made a subtle rubbing motion that would look like I was looking for something in that pocket to anyone else but him.

It worked because as we exited onto the field and the players started running ahead, Levi got in step with me and muttered, "Tease," before he ran past me to join his team. He sounded annoyed, and it felt like a win because even though we had just fucked during half-time, I knew our fighting days were not even close to being behind us.

levi

I WASN'T sure if it was the sex, or the win, but I left the stadium feeling lighter than I had in weeks. I didn't even call Rhys to go spar, and instead, headed straight home to relax after the game.

Charleigh called a good game.

I would like to think that was the sex, but I knew she had been calling a good game even before that. I was just too strung out to see things the way she did. The coach in my ear kept reminding me to keep my cool every time she threw the flag in the second half, but not once did I think I needed to take her for some spectacles.

So maybe the sex helped me, not her. But if that was the key, I needed to ensure we did that before every game.

Walking into my penthouse, I could smell tomatoes and garlic, and my nose took me straight to the kitchen. Rhys was shirtless, with his back to me, and his head bent over into a cookbook. He hadn't even realized I had come in.

"Aw, honey, you didn't have to do this for me," I teased him, making him jump from where he had been lost in the book.

"Fuck off. I got tired of eating out, and I found this cookbook in the top of the pantry." He angled his head back to the words. He had the cookbook my mom gave me when I went to college. It was supposed to be filled with cheap and easy recipes, but Rhys was making it look hard.

There were four pots on the stove, two looking like they may boil over, and the counters were trashed. I got up behind him to look over his shoulder and tried to figure out what had him so confused.

"It says I need minced garlic, but I got whole garlic and I don't know how to mince," he explained.

A laugh I hadn't let out in a while escaped and Rhys turned around to look at me with concern. "Try a knife, bozo."

"Are you okay? Did you finally lose it?"

"No." I turned from his scrutiny and pulled a beer from the fridge. "Just feels good to win."

"Holy shit, you got laid." How the fuck did he know that? And how was that making me feel lighter? Maybe I just really was happy we won.

"Nope," I lied. But that was pointless, because as I watched Rhys give up and throw whole cloves of garlic into a pot, I could tell by the smirk on his face that he didn't believe me.

"Nothing calms a man down more than pussy. Good pussy. The kind you walk away from and still think about hours later, maybe even days." *Months*, I thought to myself. Charleigh had the kinda pussy that still had me thinking of New York like it truly was the "concrete jungle where dreams are made."

"Okay, so I had sex. I'm not a kid, I have a lot of sex. It's not a big deal."

"Correct." He turned and crossed his arms over his chest, leaning against the counter to eye me better. "Except you were a lunatic before halftime. I watched the game. So, my question is, what happened at the half?"

My eyes gave me away, but the way my jaw dropped at his

observation was the nail in my coffin. He laughed again and returned to his cookbook, while I sat there and had an inner panic attack that I wasn't as sneaky as I thought.

"Relax," he said over his shoulder. "I'm your brother, and probably the only person who could figure that out so easily. Besides, I was just guessing that you got laid. Had you kept denying it, I would have believed you."

I set my bottle on the counter and sighed in defeat. I left the kitchen, hoping he was successful with the food and called me when it was ready, but not able to stand in there and answer any more of his questions.

If I was going to tell anyone how fucked up I was for fucking the ref during halftime, it would be my brother. I trusted him with my life. But the truth being said out loud meant that I would be admitting I was acting like an adolescent with no self-control or morals. That was a harder truth for me since I had to act every day like I had my shit together.

When I climbed from my shower, my phone was buzzing on my bed and I walked slowly over to answer it. No one called me on a Sunday night, so I sighed, expecting one of the players to have gotten in trouble while celebrating.

Looking down, I blew a breath of relief when I saw Al's name pop up. He was probably wondering where I was since the last few games I had ended up at his place for a fight.

"Hey Al," I answered.

"Where the hell are you?" he barked, making me smile at his predictability.

"Home, I'm fucking tired tonight."

"You ghosting me again like you did after your trip to New York?"

I cringed because Al was half right. After being introduced to Charleigh's pussy, I held back on fighting in the ring and didn't show up to Al's until she showed back up in my life. Now I could still feel how tight she squeezed my dick only hours ago and again didn't feel the need to fight.

Huh?

"Nah, I had meetings with the owner and the bruises on my face weren't a good look." That was the truth and something I needed to be mindful of.

"So should I tell Sisco you don't want a rematch?"

Why the fuck would I want to fight Sisco again?

I didn't.

But I guessed if I had lost, I would want a rematch too. Sisco seemed like the kinda guy who needed that rematch. Who was I to puss out on another fight?

"Hell, I'll fight him again. But let's make it before the bye week, so if I end up with bruises, I can hide during our week off." I knew that sounded like a pussy answer, scared of bruises, but I had to keep Richard and the rest of the front office suits off my back.

"You got it. Bobby told me the gym was always empty on Friday nights, and he was the only one usually there, so if you wanted to work out where the fight would happen, he said you're always welcome."

"I'm gonna take a couple of days to recoup from the season opener and will be back in the gym before I leave town on Saturday. The bye week is in four weeks so just let Bobby know I'm busy until then."

"Sure thing, *Brett*," Al laughed as he hung up. He may have thought it was funny, but he understood my need for anonymity. He also knew that if anyone caught on, I would have to stop paying the hefty gym fees and he didn't want that at all. I practically kept his gym open all by myself.

It wasn't as destitute as Bobby's gym, but when I went looking for a place to spar, I couldn't exactly waltz into a five-star gym and ask to butt heads with everyone. No, I had to seek out Al's, someplace lesser known and with people that I could trust.

I tossed my phone onto the bed and got dressed just as Rhys was yelling that dinner was done. I hoped like hell it tasted good, even without the garlic being minced. I also hoped Rhys would stick around for a while longer. Not so he could cook me dinners or call me out about when I have sex, but because it was nice having him around.

After the soccer season was over, he was going to be a free agent and I was going to beg him to sign with Atlanta FC. Every team in the league would be after him, the choice would be his, and I wanted him in Atlanta so bad that I wasn't above begging.

charleigh

AS THE WEEK CARRIED ON, I kept waiting for the regret to come barreling in. But it never did, and by Friday, I was convinced it never would, which didn't make sense because what I did would end my career before it ever got started.

I kept waiting on the league to call me and tell me I was fired, that Coach Peyton called and reported the incident. When that didn't happen, I kept waiting for Richard Elder to call me and tell me he owned me. But that never happened either.

"Hey Kid," Bobby called for me as I was putting my gloves on for the speed bag. "If you're gonna be around, can you lock up for me later? I wanna head into town and have drinks with an old buddy."

I looked around and noticed there were only four people in the gym. Bobby obviously had a better Friday night social life than I did because he had actual plans. Meanwhile, I was excited just for the peace.

"You know it," I nodded.

He saluted me and headed out, leaving me to assess once again who was in the gym. Three men and one woman on various equipment, all of whom usually bailed before I did anyway.

Once they all left, I would just lock up and finish my work out without worrying about anyone else coming in. Plus, it was safer that way since we weren't exactly in a safe part of town. Bobby almost never left me alone at night in the gym, so whoever he was meeting must have been someone special. I bet his "old Buddy" was promising him more than just drinks.

I wasn't judging. I was jealous.

For almost an hour, I got lost in the speed and heavy bags, feeling lighter and lighter with each punch. I could go longer, punch for days, and never get tired, but when I looked up and realized I was alone, I decided to lock up before I kept going.

Tearing my gloves off, I made my way to Bobby's office and pulled his keys out. I made my way back to the lobby and toward the door but was stopped short when I realized I was no longer alone.

Standing about five feet inside the front door, looking around like a lost puppy, was none other than Levi Peyton. He was dressed in gym shorts and a t-shirt, carrying a bag like he had the last time he was at Bobby's. *Gloves.* He was here to hit something or someone.

"Everyone's gone," I finally spoke, making him turn to see me standing by Bobby's office door.

"Yeah, Bobby said it was dead on Fridays, and I could work out without being bothered."

Bobby definitely didn't tell me to be on the lookout for *Brett.* Why the hell would he not tell me?

"Okay then," I nodded and walked to the door. "Mind if I lock us in? Rough neighborhood and all."

I was hoping he would see that I had been ready to lock up and decide to leave, but instead, he smirked and motioned for me to pass by him and head to the door. I didn't want to show him how rattled I was with him being in my space again, so I straightened my shoulders and walked past him with confidence.

After I locked the door, I tossed the keys on the counter and pointed to them. "When you get done, let yourself out." I turned to walk back to my bags, ignoring how I could sense his eyes on me the same way I had in the corridor after we had sex.

When I got my gloves back on and started swinging, he made his own move over to the ring and walked around it like it had a secret passage in the floor. From the corner of my eye, I could tell he was judging the ropes, and how worn down they were, maybe even scoffing at the mat for being so torn up. He hadn't had a lot of time when he was last there to really take in how run-down Bobby's was. I was betting myself that it was only a matter of minutes before he got spooked and made his way out the door.

"This isn't the Ritz," I yelled, not being able to help myself. The need to defend what Bobby had was ingrained in me. Those of us from that neighborhood were thankful for the shitty equipment Bobby provided for us.

Levi didn't answer me, just dropped his bag and pulled his gloves out. Seemed he had a point to prove. On the outside, I rolled my eyes, but on the inside, the butterflies in my stomach took off as I realized he was staying and we were alone.

"I'm not sleeping with you," I blurted, cringing at how pathetic I sounded.

He stopped and looked at me, making me stop and turn toward him. "That wasn't my plan, but it seems strange that you dropped your panties for me during halftime, but alone on a Friday night is where you draw the line."

"That was a mistake, and you know it," I tried to reason with him.

"Admittedly, that was not my best idea, but I haven't felt the anguish of remorse yet."

If I tried to tell him I had, he would see right through me, so I turned and started hitting the bag again. He let me be, leaving me to my own demons while he chose a bag a few down from me and started punching.

He started soft, almost getting a feel for the weight and the way it swung. After a few minutes, he was punching harder, grunting, and in a zone of concentration I wasn't even sure I could penetrate. I knew that zone, it was the one I got in when I needed to let loose.

I wanted to know what it was that made Levi feel that need. What was it that sat so deep inside of him that punching and fighting was an outlet for him? Sure, some guys just did it for a workout and enjoyed the thrill. But that wasn't what his issue was. It was more than that. More than a high-pressure coaching job, the media in his face, and everyone always in his business. It was more than the fact that he slept with me and made his job harder. It was more than anything that was obvious.

If I had never seen him fight, I would truly think he was fucking with me to control me like Richard Elder had implied in my ear the other day. But before Levi barreled into my locker room and demanded I tell him what Richard had said to me, I had seen him fight.

It wasn't the fight of a man looking for shits and giggles. It was the fight of a man who had a lot of fight in him. And that alone was what made me feel that he and I were on the same side of a fucked up and crooked world, brought together by people who only cared about the bottom line.

Did I trust him? No. But I knew when he told me to face the wall and let him fuck me that it wasn't for me to get my head on right, it was for him. He was the one who needed the outlet and he found it in me, just like I was sure he had in New York.

Backing away from my bag, I tore my gloves off and grabbed another set to hit the heavy bag with. Levi was still in his zone, so I watched him from behind, the sweat coming through his t-shirt and clinging to his back. His movements were skilled beyond boxing. He was an athlete all around. That much was obvious. I knew he had once played football, but I bet he played everything growing up–probably the best at everything as well.

"If you want to watch, why not stand behind this bag and give it more support?" he grunted.

"What, so you could miss and hit me? No thanks."

He stopped punching and turned to look at me. "I don't miss."

"But you didn't say you wouldn't punch me." I raised an eyebrow and smirked at him.

He put his hands on his waist and shook his head. "No. I didn't."

I feigned shock and took a few steps closer. "You'd hit a girl?"

"Didn't say that either." He took two steps closer to me, lessening the distance between us even more.

"Then just me? I'm special?"

"You're not a girl," he took two more steps. "I'd never do the things I did to you, to a girl."

"Oh, you mean demeaning me and using my gender against me as an argument for your team playing shitty?"

His laugh was loud, real, and completely unexpected. He licked his lips, trying not to smile and looked down at the floor while something ran through his head. I waited for his response, too curious if he was going to try and defend himself against the unwarranted things he'd said to me on the field.

"Yeah, I should probably stick with poor eyesight and insanity as to why you make the calls you do."

"Wow! So, you agree?"

"Of course, I agree. I know when I am stooping too low."

We were now two feet from one another, both of us standing with our hands on our hips and our eyes squinted at one another.

"I don't know if that makes it better or worse."

He shrugged and licked his lips. "Doesn't matter, Apple. I won't stop. Not until you're off that field."

Without thinking, I reared back with my gloved hand and punched him in the stomach. I hit him hard, making him suck in a deep and unexpected breath. But no matter how strong of a woman I was, I barely made an impact on him.

Anger coursed through me as I wished I was bigger and stronger, enough to land him on his ass and laugh as I walked away. Bringing my other hand up, I started to swing at him again, only that time, he saw it coming. He held his own glove up and blocked it before dipping down and picking me up over his shoulder with ease. I screamed, scared at first, but it quickly turned into annoyance as he climbed the steps to the boxing ring.

He set me down, placed me inside the ropes, and climbed through them himself before standing in front of me. His shoulders were huffing up and down, his face a mask of his own anger being directed back at me.

"What the hell are you doing?" I yelled.

"You threw the first punch, Apple. If you wanna fight, we can fight. Right here." He pointed his gloved hand toward the middle of the ring and raised one eyebrow to taunt me.

I started to roll my eyes and tell him I was not fighting him. But he had a point. I threw the first punch. I started this and I couldn't find my way out of it while keeping my dignity.

"Okay." I beat my gloves together. "Let's do this!"

His face almost fell, not happy with my answer. Good, let him hit me back. The pain would probably feel good.

Taking both hands, I pushed them against his t-shirt covered chest and into the middle of the ring. He backed up with ease and positioned himself in a defensive stance. He didn't look ready to punch. He looked ready to block.

levi

IF SHE THOUGHT I was going to hit her, she was delusional. Not because I didn't want to sometimes punch the mouth off of her, because I did. But I knew I was two feet taller and ten times stronger. She was mighty but small, and sometimes, her DNA and genetic makeup outbalanced her willpower. I wouldn't have even to try to fight, and I knew I would hurt her. I could think of other ways to shut her up than to punch her in the mouth.

But I wasn't lying to her. I was going to keep giving her as much hell as I could on that field until she folded. After the game last week, I realized it was just the only way. She was tough, and I found it to be a fucking turn on, but I knew eventually, she would get tired of being the joke, and bail.

In the meantime, if she needed to punch me, I was going to let her. I could fight fair and let her have a few wins, just as long as her wins were not on the field. In the ring, I was all hers.

"Come on," I said to her. "Let's fight."

She stood up from her fighting stance and backed away into the corner. "You're not going to fight me, are you?"

I stood up straight and looked confused. Did I not just tell her to fight me?

"You were in a defensive stance," she sighed. "Your only plan was to block my punches."

Fuck, she knew her shit. "Fair is fair," I shrugged.

"How is that fair?"

"I told you. I'm not gonna quit giving you excessive shit on that field. But here in the ring, you can have some punches."

"That doesn't even make sense!" she yelled. "So what if we've fucked, Levi! That doesn't mean you have to be a dick. We can both do our fucking jobs."

"That's not–" I started to somehow explain myself without even knowing the answer myself. Luckily, she cut me off before I made something up that I would later regret. The bad part was her answering words hit below the belt and I wasn't prepared.

"It's Richard, isn't it? He's making sure you run me off the field, isn't he? All that talk about being supportive of a female on the sideline, calling the game, and making it easy for me to stay in Atlanta, my hometown. It's all bullshit for the commissioner's sake, isn't it? But if I fail, the commissioner won't be so quick to put women back in my job."

I shook my head "no" before letting out a loud, "Fuck," that echoed throughout the gym. "What did he say to you?"

"You already know!"

"I told you I didn't. I have my own reasons for wanting you gone, I don't need Richard to tell me to do shit."

"What is your reason? Because we fucked?" Without letting me answer, she started to walk away. "You know what? I don't want to know."

I grabbed her gloved hand and pulled her into my chest, putting us face to face. Both of us were breathing hard, and she had every reason to hate me. Hell, I hated myself too. But I couldn't tell her the truth, and she knew fucking her had nothing to do with it. She knew we were both handcuffed to the attraction that started between us at the bar in New York. That was why she looked at my lips while licking her own. It was why her body was becoming soft and compliant as I held her against me.

"It doesn't really matter, anymore. What's done is done," I whispered. "So there isn't any reason to stop."

I closed my mouth over hers and she gave in instantly. I didn't know what she truly thought about our whole fucked up situation at work, but we both knew keeping our hands to ourselves was impossible.

We both had gloves on, so I used one on the back of her head to keep her lips on mine in case she thought about running. Not until her glove reached around and pressed into my back did I chance pulling my mouth away from hers to use my teeth on my gloves.

While I tore at the Velcro around my wrist, her mouth went to my neck, tasting the sweat that still lingered on my body. With a free hand, I was able to remove the second glove quickly and once my fingers were able to wrap around her hair, I took control.

Tugging her ponytail, I positioned her mouth in front of me and stared into her eyes. "Doesn't matter? Does it?" I asked vaguely.

"Guess not," she seethed back. She was still angry, but she had no intention of stopping the path we were about to take.

Using the control I had, I pushed her to her knees and held onto her head tightly. I made her look up at me, telling her with my eyes what I wanted her to do. She raised her gloves up, asking for help taking them off but I wanted to see her struggle.

"Figure it out, baby." If she wanted to, she would make it work, which somehow eased my conscience when it came to how big of an asshole I was with her. I just couldn't help it. She made me crazy.

She narrowed her eyes at me, not happy I was toying with her, but not pulling away either. With her gloves, she tugged at the front of my shorts the best she could, getting frustrated with how much harder it was not having her hands free. I was equally as frustrated, but not enough to not enjoy watching her try harder and harder to get to my dick.

When she finally got my shorts down low enough, I pulled her head toward me. She opened her mouth, taking me in as far as she could. Her moan vibrated with me inside her mouth and although I was ashamed to admit it, I almost came down her throat then and there.

Her gloved hands were holding steady on my thighs, so I pumped myself at my own pace, being sure she knew I was still in control. Her eyes made contact with mine, looking desperate. It made me smile devilishly. If only she understood she had the same effect on me. That I was so desperate for her that all she had to do was say the words and I would drop to my knees for her as well.

Just thinking about tasting her again made me stop my movements and zone out. She took control, moving up and down, sucking like she was getting water through a coffee stick and hadn't had a drink in days.

I needed her to stop. I needed to get my control back. Without meaning to, I pushed her too hard, making her fall back on the mat of the ring. She landed hard on her back, but I knew if I didn't get her off of me, our boxing match wouldn't end the way I wanted it to.

Squatting down, I balanced myself and rested my forearms on my knees. My dick was still out, bouncing between my open legs. "Almost forgot how good you are at that."

Her face morphed from confusion to satisfaction, feeling proud of herself with my compliment. As she sat up, I took my hand and pulled her by the neck. With me crouched down and Charleigh on her knees, we were face to face, allowing me access to her lips again.

We kissed a lot in New York, but everything was so sexually

charged that I didn't get to soak in how good it felt to really kiss her. Her mouth was heaven, and as much as I knew I needed to keep that night about sex and fighting, I couldn't help but take a minute to memorize every swipe of her tongue and movement of her lips.

She pulled back before I was ready, and used her mouth to start undoing her gloves, so I stopped her and held her wrists tight. "You have to keep these on."

Once again, she looked confused. "Is that a kink of yours?"

I smiled at her suggestion and decided that it was probably a new kink for sure. "One of us has to keep the gloves on so that this is an official fight."

"I don't want to fight." She sounded needy and like she didn't care how it made her sound, as long as she got what she wanted.

"We have to because we aren't Brett and Apple. We are Charleigh and Levi, Coach and Ref, Al's and Bobby's. Sworn enemies who should be fighting instead of fucking."

"Stop being dramatic. We can do both."

I laughed and started to crawl over her, making her lean back until she was lying flat on the mat. I hovered and settled between her open legs, grinding myself onto her covered pussy. It was a tease to both of us, but I rubbed until her eyes started to roll back in her head.

When I stopped and pulled away, she looked at me like laser beams were cutting holes into my skin. I pulled her shorts and panties down quickly so that I didn't lose her for too long. I wanted to keep her right on the edge.

Then I shed my t-shirt which was still wet from the sweat. She gave me an appreciative gleam that almost made me blush. She had seen me shirtless enough to be unaffected, but if she lusted after me the way I did her, then she would probably never be fully immune.

I let her have her fill as I took my fingers to her core. I needed to feel her, taste her, and test my memory. I pushed one finger inside of her and curled it instantly, just to see if that spot I found in New York was still hot. Based on how hard she moaned, I knew I had hit the jackpot.

"It's been three months, four now, actually. Who else has had this pussy since then?" That was a dangerous question because if she chose violence and told me someone else had touched her, I would not be able to hide my rage. Not that I had any claim to her, but she certainly felt like mine. I also needed to know if she had been as hard up as I had been since that night.

She was staring back at me, not answering my question but smirking at the fact that I asked. She was looking right through me, and I knew no matter what she said, I wouldn't like the answer. I just wouldn't know if it was the truth or a lie.

"Three," she whispered. "I go out once a month to hotels and find one-night stands. Someone who looks like they can show a girl a good time. They buy me a tequila, we laugh about his room or mine, and then fuck each other until one of us falls asleep."

I had stopped moving my finger while she told me her little tale, a short recount of New York. She bucked against my hand, trying to get me to start again, but too much ire had coursed through my blood to move. Just like I suspected, I couldn't tell if she was telling me the truth, or a lie, but it had the desired effect.

I took a second finger and pushed back into her, hard enough to make her cry out in pain instead of pleasure. "Oh, my little Apple gets around, huh? A sure-fire plan?" I was pumping my fingers in and out of her, making it hard for her to answer me. "So, I was Mr. May? Do you keep a calendar? Are there pictures for each month?"

Fuck, I was losing my goddamn mind, but I didn't know how to stop. Even knowing there was a chance she was just trying to rile me up, I was letting her. I had to turn it back around, so I brought her as close to an orgasm as I could and pulled my hands from her body abruptly.

"Ahhhh," she used her gloves to pound the floor beneath her as she cried out her frustration. I stood above her and looked down, letting her think I was finished and leaving, but I wasn't that big of a masochist. I wasn't leaving until my cum was dripping from her pussy and she was officially calling me Mr. September, October, and November.

"Get up." I said the words, but they were unnecessary since I reached down and pulled her up myself. I pushed her into the corner of the ropes and her arms opened on the top one, resting her gloves like she was in the middle of rounds.

I got up to her and pulled her tank top over her head, along with her bra. I took her shoes off too, hoping she felt more vulnerable without them. I didn't stop until she was completely naked except for her gloves. Then, I stepped back and officially lost the war.

She had a smirk on her face that told me she knew she won, but I didn't give a fuck. I threw my shorts to my ankles and lifted her legs up with my forearms. I drove my dick into her harder than I did my fingers, almost hoping I made her bleed.

Why was I like that with her? Why did she bring a monster out of me?

"Mine," I growled, like the beast I felt like. "My pussy, Charleigh."

Her head was thrown back. Her eyes were closed. She used her gloves to try to keep her upright, but I had a strong enough hold on her that she wasn't going anywhere.

"Harder!" she screamed, almost making me lose my rhythm. Harder? I was fucking her so hard I was already assuming she wouldn't be walking tomorrow. I slowed down instead, not willing to give her what she wanted. I moved slower and slower, making her look up at me and watch me.

"You don't get what you want until I get what I want," I seethed.

"What do you want?"

"Your pussy, and no one else can have it."

"But what about my calendar?"

charleigh

WHO KNEW a little lie would make Coach so mad? Then again, it didn't take much to get him fired up. Served him right for making me keep the gloves on.

But on my last words about my calendar, I couldn't keep the laugh out of my tone, and he officially knew I was fucking with him.

"Your pussy, Charleigh. Whenever I want it," he repeated, not changing his request.

"And if I say no?"

"You won't."

"No," I shot at him just to spite him.

Even though I denied him, he sped back up to his punishing rhythm, hitting places in my body no other man had ever come close to. His mouth covered mine as we both got closer and closer to our climax. When our lips were together, we couldn't talk or snarl at each other. All we could do was feel, and it was all I needed to let my defenses down and shatter in his arms.

"Levi," I moaned, wanting to say his name as I came. He loved his name coming from my mouth and even though we were in some weird battle of wills, I wanted to please him just the same.

"That's it, baby. Say it again."

"Levi," I whispered into his ear. "Levi," I said again, that time a scream.

He started jerking into me, his cock seeming to become even harder than it was moments before. He held my body in place while he pumped himself through his own orgasm. Just for good measure, I held onto his neck and leaned into his ear one more time.

"Levi," I whispered before licking his ear. His answering growl made butterflies flip around in my stomach and my heart started beating too wildly. I was feeling too much, and that wasn't what it was supposed to be about.

Thankfully, he pulled away from me and laid on his back in the middle of the ring. I pulled my gloves off and started reaching for my shirt, but he grabbed my wrist and pulled me down next to him.

Together, we lay side by side, catching our breaths.

"I have to rematch Sisco in this ring and I just want to give you a heads up that I fully plan on being knocked out cold."

"Why is that?"

"Because this ring will no longer be associated with fighting for me."

"I thought that was what we were doing, though. Fighting?"

He laughed and ran a hand through his hair. "I'm not talking about the way *we* fight."

"Well, just so we are clear, I don't have a calendar, or men to fill it up with."

"I know. You wouldn't be such a lousy ref if you were getting laid regularly."

I sat up quickly, ready to fight with him all over again. "You're an asshole. I'm fucking good at my job."

He shrugged and laughed like he hadn't just insulted me. "You called a better second half last weekend, that's for sure."

"You sorry piece of..." I trailed off, making my way on top of him and using my bare fist to try hitting his face. He grabbed my wrists and held on as I squirmed to get free, trying to imagine what his boss would say when he had new bruises that weekend.

We were both naked, so my pussy, and a culmination of our cum started to smear on his stomach. At first, I didn't notice but when I did, just the thought made me want to fuck him all over again. It was weird, going from fight to fuck, back to fight, and then back to fuck again. I couldn't keep up with my emotions.

I stopped moving, trying to let him think I was over it, but the stillness only allowed him to push his pelvis up enough to show me how hard he was again. I had almost forgotten how virile Levi was–always ready when I was back in New York.

He hesitantly let my wrists go and moved his hands to my hips. He started pushing and pulling me, back and forth, my clit finding friction on his abs. We both stayed quiet but gave in as I used his body to pleasure my own.

After a few minutes, I lifted to my knees to raise myself above him and he aligned his cock with me once again. I slowly slid down onto him, staying as quiet as I could. Even Levi was silent despite how good we both felt when we connected.

Placing my hands on his chest, I started moving, staying slow until I couldn't take it anymore. Once I started speeding up, keeping quiet was harder for us both. Moans echoed around the gym, reminding me we were on the dirty mat, with dirty bodies from our workouts.

"Mine," Levi said again, the way he did during round one.

We both immediately let go, coming again like it was the first time ever between us. Every time felt like that first time. A blast of something prodigious, but nothing we could explain, or put into words. Nothing we ever even mentioned. But it was there in New York, there in my locker room, there in the corner of the ring, and there on that mat as we let ourselves soak in that sensation.

I tried rolling off of Levi, but he held me in place and sat up. We were face to face again, breathing heavily. It seemed too intimate for two people who were supposed to be fighting, but I was trapped in his gaze.

When his breathing slowed, he pushed me back and held himself inside of me while he lifted us both from the mat. It was a true show of his strength and that he was definitely an athlete. I wrapped my legs around him, and he made his way out of the ring, under the ropes, and down the steps. He held on tight, making sure his cock stayed securely inside of me until we were in the men's locker room.

Just a couple of weeks before, we stood face to face in that locker room and barely knew what to say to one another. Now we were intertwined and connected, neither trying to let the other go.

Levi carried me straight into the showers and turned the cold water on over our heads, a screech coming from us both as we adjusted. Finally, he let me slide down his body and onto my feet. He grabbed some body wash, and though I wasn't even sure where it came from, it was welcomed after being on the dirty mat.

He lathered the soap into his hand and quietly cleansed my body as I watched on in awe. It was another moment of intimacy that was deeper than even New York gave us. I wondered if he even realized what was happening or how it felt.

I had to make sure I didn't fall into a trap of lust that was blurred by lines we never discussed, only ones we knew we couldn't cross. Levi was right, though. When the gloves were on, it felt like a fight–safer, easier to forget. Once my gloves were off, it was more, and that scared me into backing away from his hands under the cascade of water.

"What's wrong?" he asked, his hands in the air and soap dripping from them.

"Nothing, I just figured now that we have had our fun it's time to get back to business."

His face fell slightly, but he recovered. His soapy hands started rubbing his own body and I watched on as he lathered his cock and stroked himself clean. "Well go ahead and run then, Apple Parks. Knowing I can have that pussy whenever I want makes it easier to say good night."

I tilted my head. "I never agreed to that."

"You may not have said the words, but you agreed."

"You're delusional if you think you can snap your fingers and I will come running with a wet pussy." I said *those* words, but I didn't even believe myself. I knew if he called, I would go running, and shed my clothes as I went.

He turned the shower off and grabbed a towel, wiping himself dry. I stood there with my arms crossed, looking put off by his suggestion. He smiled at me, but he never said another word. When he was all dry, he tossed the towel at me and walked off.

"See you Sunday," he turned back and smiled at me before opening the door to head naked into the gym. "During halftime," he added, his suggestion dripping heavily.

I started to yell, "*No*," that if he was implying he could have me whenever he wanted me, then no, I said no. But deep down, I was already trying to remember if the female official's locker room was near the visiting team's corridor in Chicago. If it would be easy to pull him into my space and have him bend me over the couch.

It took me entirely too long to steel myself against anything happening between us on our trip to Chicago. By the time I left the locker room, he was long gone. He had grabbed his clothes and let himself out of the gym while I walked around naked, praying Bobby never sprung for those cameras he talked about a few months back.

levi

THERE WERE two away games Charleigh would be officiating during the regular season. Chicago and Las Vegas. She had a few more out-of-town games, but those were the two she would be officiating that the Jets would be playing. For some reason, I felt my anxiety lessen, knowing she was close to me, but not in Atlanta.

I had kept my cool for most of the game against Chicago, barely raising my voice. It also helped that we were up by two touchdowns, and that Charleigh was assigned to the home team side of the field, which meant she was not the line judge standing in my way.

The unfortunate part was that Chicago had her locker room down the home team corridor, and I wasn't going to be able to sneak into her locker room at halftime to fuck her senseless like I had promised. I was, however, sure that I was going to track her down right after the game and make up for the lost time.

It'd been two days since we were in the gym and I hadn't seen her since. She had obviously taken her own flight because why would an official fly with the team? It seemed as though she was at a different hotel as well. Not that I stayed in the lobby all night waiting for her to arrive or anything.

I had spent the entire first half against Chicago glancing at her across the field before eyeing my team's next play. It had become somewhat of a habit. Call the play, adjust the play, watch the guys get in position, glance up at Charleigh, and then get my head back in the game.

You'd think I knew at that moment how fucked I was, but it was well into the second half before things finally cracked.

As the game dwindled down, timeouts and stopped plays were happening in excess. All I wanted was for the game to end so badly that I had shed my headset altogether. I was pacing along the line on the field, waiting for the clock to hit zero so I could march across and tell Charleigh to drop her fucking pants.

That was when I knew I was fucked.

I cared more about getting to Charleigh than I did the game. I didn't know what to do with that spinning around in my head. I didn't even like Charleigh, did I? I liked Apple. Apple was funny, intelligent, witty, charming... Apple was Charleigh, though.

"Coach? Let's go." My assistant was pushing me onto the field to go shake hands with the opposing team as I stood there wondering if I hated Charleigh or not. As I jogged toward the center of the field, I decided I didn't hate fucking Charleigh, and that was good enough for me.

"Good game, Coach," I said as I shook hands with my opponent.

"See you in a few weeks," he smiled back.

We had another game against Chicago at home right after our bye week, and I knew they would be out for revenge. I made a mental note to watch the last five minutes of the game over and over again, because I had been watching Charleigh and they probably made adjustments that would kick our ass next time.

More proof I was making a huge mistake by hunting her down. But I had a plan. Find her, fuck her, and make it back to the locker room with my team before anyone starts to wonder where I was.

After my handshake, I told my assistant coaches I was headed to say hello to a few people and would catch up later. They left me alone, and I started toward the home team corridor. Black and white stripes caught my eye and I saw the long braid Charleigh wore so I followed her as discreetly as possible–even though she was going extremely fast.

In my own stadium, it was a risk. In an away stadium, it was career suicide. But when I thought about New York and all the low points since that trip, I needed the adrenaline that chasing her gave me. But that was the only time I would do it, and I knew it would be out of my system.

Just like in our stadium, there was a turn into a secluded area where Charleigh had run to. I made the next few paces, keeping my head low in hopes no one would recognize me. Odds were good that no one would be looking for me over there and wouldn't pay me any attention, but I kept low just in case.

Once I turned into the corner that Charleigh did, I was relieved to see it was set up like ours. A small hall and a door that anyone passing by wouldn't be able to see me go into. I raised my hand to knock but decided just to barge in instead, hoping to grab the upper hand on whatever fight she wanted to put up.

I tried the handle, and it didn't turn. A sigh of relief had settled through me because I mentally berated her more than once for not locking the door back at home. Any motherfucker could walk right in–like me.

I knocked hard and then placed my hands on either side of the doorframe, listening as I heard her move around on the other side of the door. I didn't have much time, but part of the thrill for me was seeing how fast I could make her come. Still, she needed to open the fucking door.

I knocked one more time, and slowly, the door finally opened. Her eyes peeked out in a reserved manner, but when she saw it was me, she opened the door all the way.

Pushing my way in, I quickly and instantly shoved her into the wall. My hand wrapped around her throat as I started rubbing her pussy on the outside of her pants.

"I missed you at halftime," I whispered but left the agitation in my voice.

"I missed you too." Her words were broken, emotional, and my eyes shot up to hers for the first time since I walked in.

Her eyes were glassy, and her face was red. She had already taken her hat off, so I had a clear view as I searched for what was wrong. I started to pull my hand away, but she stopped me, holding it to her neck and keeping her eyes on me. "Don't stop."

I moved my other hand again, rubbing her pussy as I watched her face morph from rigid to lustful. Something was wrong, and even though I shouldn't care, I also didn't want to take advantage of her. I may have been a little rough with her, but she always wanted it. Her being upset while I still held her up was making me question my morals.

"I need it," she croaked, seeing me at war with myself. "Just like when we fought the other night, Levi. So hard it hurts."

I brought my hand up and popped her pants open then reached my hand down to feel if she was even wet. Somehow, through whatever she was going through, she was soaked, and my dick stood at attention.

"Fucking hell," I gritted, still not sure I was doing the right thing. But I pulled her up from the wall only to slam her back into it out of frustration.

I started using my middle finger to rub her clit, faster and faster, hoping to bring her to the brink quickly. As soon as she started trembling, I pulled my hand away and went down to my knees.

I pulled her shoes off, followed by her black pants and lacy panties. The lace made me slightly pissed that she had been on the other sideline all day wearing those without me being behind her to look at her ass.

Charleigh pulled her own shirt over her head, leaving her naked as she looked down at me on my knees. It was the complete opposite of the other night in the ring. Instead of looking down at her, I looked up, and it felt like a power change.

Despite the fact that I came in blazing, she was the one in charge. I waited for a second before I turned my hat backward, letting her know I was about to taste her with just that motion. I picked her left foot up and placed it on my shoulder. Leaning in, I took my tongue between her folds and lapped at the wetness I had elicited with my fingers.

Charleigh grabbed the side of my head and held on to keep herself steady and to keep me close. I tasted and played with her, used my memory from New York to lick and bite every spot I knew would make her knees weak. Without meaning to, I started moving my own pelvis, seeking friction against my own pants like a fucking teenager. I needed her to touch me so badly, but I couldn't bring myself to pull away.

The TV in the background of the room caught my attention though. *"We are just waiting on Coach Peyton to join us so he can break down the game for us."*

She and I both gasped at the same time from the words of the announcer, but I didn't stop. I was already there, hard and ready to fuck her senseless. "They can wait," I told her.

I licked her a few more times, then closed my mouth over her clit, knowing it would make her explode. She started shaking again, the way she did when she came, and her moans were unintelligible. My mouth stayed on her until I was sure she had come down from her orgasm, then I stood up and lowered my joggers.

Instead of driving into her while we were standing, I grabbed her by the waist and pushed her onto the couch. I hovered over her, one leg on the floor and the other smashed against the back of the couch. She spread her legs to make room for my huge frame and I pushed inside of her softly.

"Harder," she pulled at my shoulders, shaking her head back and forth so I couldn't see her eyes. "Make it hurt."

Grabbing her face, I stopped her movements. "Open your eyes."

She didn't at first, but after I shook her chin a few times, she finally opened them. A small tear ran from the corner of her eye down to her cheek and I knew I needed to back away. She was tough as nails and even though I didn't know her well enough to know if she was a crier, I knew it was rare and something major had happened.

"Harder, Levi," she demanded.

I started moving again, but only because my body reacted to her harshness. It was recognizing the fight in her and my body loved her fight.

"Harder," she said again, tilting her head back and moaning the word over and over. I let go of her chin and braced myself on the couch, going as hard as I could inside of her. Her moans turned into screams, the pain filtering its way through her body. Guilt ate away at me, but I couldn't understand why. We were always aggressive and hard with one another. Why were her tears making me weak?

Her tits bounced below me, catching my attention and I latched onto her nipple with my teeth. I bit down hard, pulling and licking as I moved to the other to do the same thing. By the time I finished tugging on her other nipple, her pussy started to clench around my dick, and I knew she was about to come. I pulled up, wanting to watch her but the ecstasy she had written on her face as her mouth hung open and her breathing labored was too much for me.

My own head tilted back, and I came as she came, hard and never seeming to end. I pumped into her until I was weak, my arms giving out as I fell on top of her. She didn't protest or even push me away. She let me lay on top of her, inside her, as my heart rate returned to normal.

When I pushed up, I looked down at her and her eyes were closed. She looked sated and blissed out, and I knew I had done the right thing by listening to her commands. I didn't know what she was feeling, but if fucking her hard helped, then I didn't have to feel guilty about pushing her while she was down.

Leaning up, I grabbed a towel that had been folded on the arm of the couch and tossed it to her before I pulled out and straightened myself up. She didn't bother cleaning herself up, or even moving, but her eyes were open watching me.

"I have to go do this interview, but Charleigh...When I see you again, I want to know what the hell happened to cause those tears."

"Don't worry about it, Coach. It's none of your fucking business."

I smirked, glad to see my girl back in her snarky form. I threw her clothes back at her and made my way toward the door. Sneaking out was easier than I expected since the corridor was practically empty. I kept my head low and made my way across the field to the visitor's side and started to walk straight to the press conference.

Right before my feet entered the room, though, I was stopped short by my own brain as it finally clicked what I had just said. Maybe not out loud, but as I left, I thought of Charleigh as *my girl*, which would create a whole new set of issues.

charleigh

LEVI PEYTON WAS one smooth talker.

Explaining to the media that he saw an old friend and got caught up chatting after the game was like watching an artist paint. The strokes of his bullshit were masterful, like happy little trees all over the damn canvas.

I laid on that spot in the locker room, naked, while I watched him walk into the press conference. The crowd started asking a bunch of questions and although he looked rattled at first, he quickly smoothed it all over.

That stunt was too dangerous. We could have gotten caught and if I hadn't seen Levi weave the tale of meeting up with an old friend with my own eyes, I would have thought getting caught was his plan. At least getting *me* caught.

His boss would wipe his transgressions away while mine would fly high as a symbol of why women didn't belong in sports. I should have been horrified, regretful, and remorseful, but just like every other time I had sex with Coach Peyton, I couldn't find it in me to feel any of those things.

Content, happy, relaxed. That was all I felt, and Levi had become my drug—a way to wipe all the stress away, if only for a little bit. Just like in the gym, I knew all he had to do was tell me to spread my legs and I would.

But something happened in Chicago that I never thought I would see. Levi was a touch submissive. He homed in on my emotions and went from lion to kitten in the blink of an eye. Unlike at the gym, he didn't falter at giving me what I wanted. He listened and gave me everything.

I had been emotional before he stepped foot in that room, but my tears were for him by the time he left. For the fact that he could set the asshole that sat on the surface of his skin aside for that moment and give me what I needed.

It was that kind of attention that a girl could get used to. It was the kind of thing that turned enemies into lovers. Something that made me let my guard down a little and want to trust him in a way I knew I shouldn't.

But after the day in Chicago, I knew I couldn't trust anyone. Not in the NFL business. There was one other female referee in the league, and she was primarily in San Francisco, so I couldn't even befriend her and pick her brain. I wondered if she dealt with the same things I had.

She was much older than I was, from what I could tell when I saw her on TV, but that didn't matter. San Francisco's coach was in his seventies and married. I giggled at myself as I pictured them running to the locker room to fuck during halftime.

Hell, I guess it didn't matter how old anyone was. I bet there was dirty shit going on all over the league. Based on the way Richard spoke to me last week, I bet he was a part of half the underhanded shit on the east coast.

I spent my entire flight home thinking of how I could avoid Richard all season. He creeped me out and made me feel little. He took no pride in having a female referee in his stadium every week. If he did, he had a weird way of showing it.

Chicago's team was certainly glad I was there. They got off on trying to belittle me as much as possible, probably hoping I faltered on a call. I was sure they were looking for any excuse to file a complaint.

Maybe condemning the whole team wasn't fair since it seemed to be just one person, but my defenses were up. Number sixty-seven for Chicago, whoever the fuck that was, almost rattled me to my core. So much so that I left the field emotional and over-whelmed.

When I finally got into my apartment, I went straight to the shower and crashed into my bed. I turned the TV onto the late-night sports shows, even though I feared their every word. Some dark part of me wanted to know what was being said, if I was being scrutinized, or if anyone was reporting how Coach Peyton snuck into my locker room.

Fortunately, it was all good things when it came to the Atlanta versus Chicago game. Coach Peyton happily did his press conference, probably because of the post-game orgasm he had. The team played well. No crazy rant about the officiating crew.

I fell asleep to the replay of the press conference, Levi's voice somehow soothing me into a state of warmth and safety. It didn't matter that he was talking football, it all sounded like sex to me, and I let myself feel that emotion for a little bit longer. I knew when I woke up for work Monday I had to let it go.

I couldn't afford to find safety in a fighter.

"Sisco and Brett are rematching," Bobby said first thing Monday. Of course, that was news we already knew, but he was sitting on his desk, his arms crossed and concern written across his face.

I instantly started panicking, wondering if he really did install the cameras and while I was out of town, he spent the weekend sifting through the porn Levi and I created in the middle of the ring.

"Yeah, so," Bond huffed.

"He wants an audience, something official."

I stood up, instantly more worried than I would be if he saw me having sex in the ring. "No!"

Bobby looked over and squinted his eyes at me. Having an audience meant money, betting, and publicity for the gym. It would be crazy for Bobby to miss that chance, but I didn't think Levi would appreciate being the center of that show.

"What's your problem, Kid? It won't be that much more work if that's what is bothering you. The boys will handle the heavy stuff."

"It's not that, I just... What did Al say? Brett?"

"Who cares what they say, this is my gym."

In that instant, I knew he had not even discussed it with Al. He was going to just set the gym up for an audience and surprise Al and Levi when they got there. It wasn't exactly underhanded where Bobby was concerned. Gyms did that all the time when it came to fights. As long as they cut Al and Levi in at a certain percentage, no one would be bothered.

Usually.

But Al knew Brett was Levi Peyton and he knew Levi wanted to keep his fighting on the down low. He wouldn't agree to exploit the fight because the more attention it got, the more likely someone would recognize Levi.

"Listen," Bobby started again. "We keep this between us. No one else in the gym can know until the day of the fight. I told Al that Brett could come in whenever he wanted to work out here, so he could show up at any moment. We don't want to spook him."

"Maybe he should be given the choice," I suggested.

"He'll be happy once he walks out of here with a few thousand in his pocket, trust me."

"Then why not just bring it up now and let him prepare for it."

Bobby's eyes squinted at me again, concerned for what I was suggesting. "Charleigh, you know how this works. Not even Sisco is gonna know that I am making this happen. It'll be a fair fight."

No, it wouldn't. Sisco asked for it and would probably be expecting it. Levi would be blindsided.

I nodded to keep my cool but left to the female locker room for a minute to myself. I paced back and forth, unsure what I should do. The right thing would be to warn Levi and let him back out of the fight. Then again, why did I care? Bobby's gym and my family at the gym meant more to me than Levi. Just because we were having sex didn't mean I started caring about him.

His face flashed in my mind, the face he gave me as he looked up at me, kneeling on the floor in Chicago. How he was worried and cared, but also mindful enough to give me what I wanted. That wasn't the face of a man I could betray.

Was it?

levi

"HOW MANY TIMES are you going to watch that play?" I looked up from my laptop, realizing Dave was behind me. I shut the computer and shrugged as he rounded to the chair in front of me and sat down. "Cam threw that ball perfectly. Ty caught it with excellent form. What is there to overanalyze?"

It wasn't the play that had me fucked up, it was what went on behind the play. Something I couldn't see from across the field until it was on my screen. Something no one else saw or would ever see because they didn't know to look for it.

"Earth to Coach," Dave laughed and leaned back, watching me like I was a side show at the circus.

"Just thinking," I gritted out, trying to suppress the fury.

"Let me guess, the sexy line judge should have thrown a flag for pass interference regardless of how well the play turned out for us."

"What the fuck are you talking about?" I didn't think the play deserved a flag, and I was confused why he was bringing it up. I also didn't like him calling Charleigh sexy any more than I liked Rhys calling her hot.

"Coach, you are out for her blood. We all see it. It's not sitting well with you when she makes calls you don't agree with."

"I always yell at the referees; it's practically in the job description."

"But I have never seen you as irate as you get with her."

I leaned back in the chair and crossed my arms, trying to figure out where he was going with his little story.

"I know that's what you're doing. You are looking for anything you can to push her off that field. I say this as a friend, not as your assistant coach, but it looks bad. You are coming across as a chauvinist."

"How the-?" I cut myself off, about to explode again.

"I'm just being the bird in your ear. You need to find a way to calm down and let her do her job without insulting her."

He had no idea what I was trying to do to Charleigh Wright. Get her off the field? Yeah, I wanted that more than I wanted anything, but not because I was a chauvinist. I had reasons well beyond that, and I wasn't sure he was ready to hear them.

"I'll keep that in mind," I seethed at him before changing the subject.

It was already Wednesday, and we had a lot of prep before our home game that weekend. The other coaches filed into the room, taking their seats, and we got busy with our daily meetings.

Dave was able to let his comments fade away and no one else brought up my behavior, but I looked around the room constantly, trying to see if there were any scrutinizing faces looking my way.

Practice went smoothly, and by the end of the day, I had almost forgotten about Dave's warning all together. But I didn't forget about the video I watched three hundred times. I didn't forget how much my fingers twitched to hit something.

I texted Rhys to see if he wanted to meet me at Al's. He had been back and forth from Atlanta to Miami to see his doctors and babysit me. His flight was supposed to land while I was at practice, so I hoped he was antsy for a fight after being stuck on a plane all day.

I leaned back in my office chair, mentally taking note of anyone who might be at Al's and would want to spar. Then I thought about Bobby's, and my open invite to workout whenever I wanted leading up to the rematch. But heading to Bobby's would probably be worse since I needed to steer clear of Charleigh. Not sure the guys there on Wednesdays could handle the way we fight.

"Coach? Got a minute?"

I looked up to see Cam walking into my office, so I sat up and tried to look less manic in the presence of my quarterback. "Sure, what's up?"

He sighed and sat down, leaning back to get comfortable in the chair that sat in front of my desk. I was surprised to see him; he was usually one of the first to leave after practice.

"I just wanted to check on you. Seems like no one else is." He looked down at his phone and thumbed a message out before he looked back up at me. "Told Kace where to find me."

I nodded, knowing his best friend Kace was always around when he could be. He was a professional baseball player for the Atlanta Kings, and they were infamous best friends. I knew all about him, and he knew enough about the Jets to know where my office was and how to get there. I imagined he would be walking in soon, so I wanted to hurry and end the conversation.

"I'm good, Nichols. What makes you ask?"

"Richard seems to be acting like a dick, Ty having his issues is stressful, your brother has been bouncing between staying with you and going home, the line judge seems to be getting under your skin, and the bruises I have seen on your face here and there have me really worried."

I bowed my head, not sure how to respond, or how upset I should be. I was glad he was concerned about me, but not one thing he mentioned was something I could talk about, except for my brother.

"Rhys is staying at my place to stay out of Miami, but he has to go back for his doctor's visits."

Cam nodded but stayed quiet, hoping I elaborated on more.

"Ty can fill you in on his trouble if he wants to, but it's not my place to say. And the rest is something I'm not sure even exists."

"Where are the bruises coming from?" His voice was deep, like that was really the only thing he wanted to ask in the first place.

I decided to tell him just a little out of the respect I had for him. I also knew he had been through quite a bit in the past year and tended to worry. I didn't need him worrying over me.

"Honestly, Cam, I started boxing as a workout, and I'm not very good at it."

His eyes narrowed in on me, trying to determine how much of what I had just said was a lie. Other than the word "boxing", it was all a lie. I hadn't just taken it up for a workout, and I was fucking good at it.

"Hey," I heard Kace's voice before I saw him walk into the office. He looked between Cam and me and started to back out, sensing there was something going on that needed to be settled. If he left, Cam would call me out on the lie I just told.

"Kace," I stood up and walked around to the front of my desk, shaking Kace's hand because it had been a while since I had seen him. "How are you?"

"Good, Coach, good. Should I give you a minute?" He glanced at Cam for his question, but Cam already started to let it all go. Kace had that effect on him. They fed off one another in a way that was rare between men. Their lifelong friendship and the fact that they shared a girlfriend, had brought them even closer. If it hadn't been for Kace, Cam might not be the wizard on the field, or the good human he was off the field.

Cam stood up hesitantly. "No, we're done. I just needed to check on Coach."

"All good, Cam. I promise."

"Come on." Kace pulled Cam by the shoulder. "Ali is at home waiting; this is our last night all together before I have to leave town again."

A little jealousy rose up every time I thought about how lucky they were to have not only each other, but someone they loved enough to hurry home to. It was always easy to forget how lonely I was until I was around some of the guys who were blissfully happy.

As they left, I sank back down in my chair and added envy to the list of things making my head spin and my body ache. Little by little, I felt like I was being chipped away at, unsure if I would ever feel the same as I used to before things got so chaotic.

How did my life become all about secrets, rage, and drama? It wasn't the day I became a coach because the feelings I had had didn't exist in previous years. I was perfectly content with my life, my job, and my future.

So, when did it all change?

I asked myself that question, but I already knew the answer. My life changed when I was summoned to New York. That one night changed my entire outlook on everything and twisted me into the madman I was.

And the craziest part was, it wasn't because of Charleigh "Apple" Wright.

charleigh

I WALKED THE SIDELINES, waiting for the game to start.

I hadn't seen Levi since Chicago, and even with us both on the field, he wasn't paying me any mind. He was focused on the team, and as much as I tried not taking that personally, it felt like a punch to my gut.

Levi was doing what he was supposed to be doing, what he should have always been doing. It was wrong of me to have hurt feelings because he couldn't even look my way, but there I was, stewing as I walked back and forth.

My officiating team was out on the field, chatting and doing what they did before each game. Maybe I should have been out there with them, but I was too in my head over everything.

All week I had been thinking about if I should tell Levi about Bobby's plans for the fight. When Friday came, I did my work out in an empty gym and waited for Levi to show up to spar. He knew I would be there, most likely alone, so I thought he would show up. I told myself if he did, I would tell him the truth.

But he didn't, and I was back to remembering that Bobby was who I should be loyal to. Levi said it himself, we are enemies, and although I know he was just being dramatic with that term, he was also serious about the meaning. So how could I even think of betraying Bobby and thwarting his plans just because Levi had a special way of making me orgasm?

"Heads up!" I heard a few people on the sidelines yell and I turned to make sure nothing was coming my way. In doing so, I ran into someone and almost fell.

"Oh my God, I'm so sorry," I said before looking up to see who I had run into.

Ali Hansen, made famous after she became involved with not only Cam Nichols, but Kace Jackson as well.

"It's okay," she smiled. "I think I get run into, or hit with something, every time I'm down here."

"I've had a few close calls, but it's getting harder to avoid," I joked. I stuck my hand out to be cordial. "Charleigh Wright."

She took my hand and her smile widened. "I know exactly who you are," she motioned to my uniform. "Ali Hansen, it's an honor to meet you."

"I know exactly who you are, too," I admitted.

Ali blushed, showing a small amount of insecurity over how she became so famous. "Yeah well, you are making waves in this world. I'm just dating the quarterback."

As if on cue, Kace came up behind her and kissed her cheek, interrupting us. "Hey baby, let's go see Cam and head to our seats. I'm starving." He looked up, finally realizing I was there and backed away. "Oh hey, Kace Jackson."

I took his outreached hand and shook, introducing myself the same way I had to Ali.

"You two enjoy the game," I nodded and started backing away. "I have to go get myself ready to make the calls."

Kace smiled and looked to Ali. "Let's hurry and see Cam. He said Coach Peyton was scaring the shit out of him, so we don't need to hang around for that. Nice meeting you, Ms. Wright. Have a good game. Good luck," he winked.

"You too," I motioned to Ali, "She said she's dating the quarterback, so you may need more luck than I do."

They both laughed at my joke, Ali turning red again before shaking her head and leaving hand in hand with Kace.

The whole interaction made me feel lighter, and happier. Like maybe there were normal people in the world who wished me well and were nice to talk to. Since starting the job, hardly anyone had held a conversation with me like that. Easy and carefree.

Kace's words crept in. *"Coach Peyton is scaring him..."*

Coach Peyton seemed like a puppy compared to the other games, how could that be scary? Or maybe that was the point. He was acting differently, and that scared the team. They sensed something was up.

"Not your problem, Charleigh," I whispered to myself.

Just like every other game, the action did not get too out of hand until right before halftime when the clock was ticking down to zero. The teams started to get aggressive, trying for a touchdown before the half. I threw four flags in the final minute alone.

Levi never said a word.

No yelling, screaming, insults, fighting, or tantrums. He stood stoic, arms crossed, legs spread. I could hear his voice talking to the other coaches in his headset, but when I glanced at him, he never even paid me any mind.

Cam was right, Coach was scary. His silence wasn't met with a docile aura, it was just magnifying the stress that simmered inside of him. A bomb ready to explode. I even started to throw a flag and make a bad call just to get a rise out of him, and ease the pressure.

"Not your problem," I whispered again to myself.

When the whistle blew for halftime, everyone started to jog to their locker rooms, me included. I slowed my trot, just to let Levi catch up to where I was, then without even looking at him, I said, "We need to talk. Now."

He stayed quiet and jogged faster, disregarding me as if he didn't even hear me. I stopped jogging and let him go, tempted to not even go to my locker room for halftime. I had water on the field, but I craved those fifteen minutes out of the eye of the crowd.

I started jogging again, making my way to my sanctuary. When I reached the corridor, Levi was long gone with his team, deeper into the tunnel. I made the turn into my little alcove and entered my room, stopping in my tracks when I realized I wasn't alone.

Closing the door, I eyed Levi as he stood against the wall with his arms crossed. I leaned on the closed door, facing him with my hands behind my back. We stared at each other for a minute before either of us spoke.

"Are you okay?" I asked.

"Is that what we need to talk about?" *So, he did hear me, he did get my message.*

"Yeah, it is. You're scaring me."

"I haven't said a word to you." His voice was angry, confused. "How the fuck am I scaring you?"

"You're not scaring me as a coach. You're scaring me as a human. Something happened."

He sighed heavily and looked to the ceiling. "I can't win, I'm tired of trying."

"Football? The Jets are up by fourteen–"

"Everything!" he yelled. "I have so much shit on my plate, so many people I have to make happy, so many people I need to piss off, and I can't concentrate on any of it."

"Do you want to talk about it?"

He looked at me like I was crazy, shaking his head and scrunching his nose. "Fuck, no. I'm not talking to anyone, much less you."

I flinched from his hatred and anger, realizing I had overstepped. Somewhere along the way, I started caring about Levi more than I should have. It probably happened when he took care of me after the game in Chicago, letting me have control.

I should have listened to myself, *that it wasn't my problem*. I should have moved out of Levi's way and told him to leave. I should have let his ire be his own downfall.

But instead, I took three long strides to stand in front of him and went down to my knees. I looked up at him like I did when we were in the middle of the ring. I tried to tell him with my eyes alone what my intentions were. He fixed me last week, so I was going to fix him this time.

His breath sucked in as I reached for the waistband of his joggers. I slowly lowered them down and opened my mouth. From the moment I knelt in front of him, he was hard, so by the time I pulled his cock out, he was ready for me.

Though I was slow with his pants, I was quick to take him in my mouth, knowing our time was limited. I kept my eyes on him as I wrapped a hand around the base that I couldn't reach with my mouth, pumping him hard and fast. I swirled my tongue, remembering the last time I sucked his cock and what I knew he liked.

He hissed, and moaned, his eyes closing as he gradually lost control. I pulled my mouth back and kept stroking with my hand while I spoke to him. "Get out of your head, Coach. I want you to go back out there and yell at me, insult me, threaten me. But don't you dare go back out there and succumb to the pressure. You have more fight in you than that."

He stared down, absorbing my words as I wrapped my mouth back around him. I took my free hand between his thighs and slightly stroked, teasing him as if I was going to touch him in other places.

The tease was all it took as he growled and started moving his hips to match my motions. He started jerking and his knees started to shake right before I tasted him on my tongue. His release was long, and I swallowed him down quickly, knowing we were out of time.

Backing away, I gave him room to pull his pants back up and adjust himself while I watched from the floor. He didn't say anything or even acknowledge what had just happened. He simply moved around me and left, slamming the door on his way out.

levi

SHE WAS RETURNING a favor and that was all there was to it.

But it worked.

With everything compounding into a level of stress that made me worry for my own pending heart attack, it felt good to have her mouth on me. Not just because of the release, but because for those few minutes, I wasn't alone.

She and I had a lot in common, with pressure that surmounted the average person in our same positions in the league. We may have been at each other's throats, but that wasn't because we didn't understand each other. It was because we were so much alike.

Our night in New York was long gone from being a part of my stress, and I was sure it wasn't an issue for her either. We had crossed way more lines than an anonymous one-night stand.

Even though I felt relieved and relaxed after halftime, I still stayed fairly quiet. I thought maybe she was worried the world would know something was going on between us if I wasn't yelling, but all my silence was supposed to be doing was protesting. More than anything, I didn't want the suits to win their war, not against me, and not against her.

I knew I would pay for my silence later, but something bigger was happening in the NFL, and I hadn't decided yet who to trust. All I knew was I was going to choose to be on the right side of things because my mother didn't raise Rhys and me out of the slums as boys for us to falter as men.

Where Charleigh was concerned, I walked a fine line that I shouldn't have crossed. But had I never made that leap, I might not have been cognizant enough to see what was happening. Now, I just needed a plan.

When the game ended, I walked past Charleigh as we made our way off the field. I slid a piece of paper into her palm, and she took it without question, walking like nothing had happened. I wasn't sure if that was part of my plan, but it was needed. I could no longer rely on just seeing and talking to her on Sundays. Getting to know her was necessary for me to know if I was doing the right thing in the long run.

You slid me your number like a middle schooler?

I've been acting kind of juvenile, huh?

What do you want?

I leaned back on my bed; thankful she hadn't waited too long to text me. After the game, I got a workout, showered, ate dinner with Rhys, and laid back to wait. It was like she knew the moment I was settled and needed to hear from her.

To fight.

With fists, words, or naked?

All three.

I smiled at our banter, picturing her rolling her eyes at me as she read my messages. It was different for us–calm, nice.

Wow, you suck a guy's dick one time, and they
get clingy.

You've sucked it more than once.

Touché.

And you will suck it again.

There you go again, assuming I will jump when
you tell me to.

Turns out, I don't even have to tell you to.

Don't make me regret it.

No regrets. We are way past regrets.

So, what do you want?

Let's fight Friday.

I bit my lip and worried I wasn't being direct enough. Could she read between the lines? Did she understand I meant more than just fuck or fight?

What do you have in mind?

Meet me at Bobby's and we go from there.

Well, you already know that's where I'll be.

> But I needed to make sure you had clothes with you, something you could change into.

The bubbles of her impending text popped up, stayed up for a while, and then disappeared. When they came back onto my screen, I held my breath and waited for her response again. But just like before, the bubbles disappeared with no messages coming through.

Finally, after what felt like a full five minutes, her answer came through.

K.

I decided to leave it at that, knowing she was probably trying to decide if meeting up with me was a good idea. It was a terrible idea, so since she said "K," I refused to read or answer any more texts until Friday. I was not taking any chances that she would come to her senses and back out.

I was actually feeling good for the first time in weeks. Having something to look forward to did that for me. Leaning back on my arms, I crossed my feet and smiled as I stared at my ceiling. I could hear Rhys talking on his phone from the living room and knew he would be distracted the rest of the night. So, I grabbed my remote and started to do something I hadn't done in a while—watch TV. Something so simple and mundane, but something I never had the time or energy for.

I was seven minutes into a rerun of CSI: Miami when I heard my phone buzz with a text on the bed next to me. Rhys was still talking on his phone, the drama with Ty had died down, and my mom chose to call rather than text, so I figured that only left Charleigh as the one to text.

She was going to change her mind and I didn't want to know about it. I should have blocked her number so her texts wouldn't tempt me. Sometimes ignorance was bliss and this was one of those times. I had ten or so minutes to think about doing something normal and sane with Charleigh and now I was going to have to go back to fighting her and fucking her.

Because doing nothing with her wasn't an option.

Lifting my phone, I sighed and opened the screen to read the text. I sat up quickly, rage coursing my veins like it tended to do when I needed to hit something. On the bright side, it wasn't Charleigh turning me down.

It was Richard, and he had just three words for me.

Time is up!

charleigh

LEVI WAS in the gym before everyone left. He had started working out as if he had always been a member of Bobby's. No one talked to him, but a few leered his way as he punched the bags hard, making dust and powder puff into the air from each hit.

His shirt was off, his shorts were tight around his muscular thighs, and his headphones were in each ear. I leaned against the ring and watched as anyone who cared what I was doing was long gone. The others were leaving the gym slowly and it was only a matter of time before we were alone.

I spent way too much time trying to decide how I was going to approach him when the final person cleared out. Would I tap him angrily and start a fight? Would I jump in front of his bag and tempt him to hit me? Or did I take a softer approach, lacing my hands around his hips and molding my body to his until he succumbed to my hold?

The last option seemed too intimate, but then again, we had recently shifted something in our relationship that felt a lot like intimacy. He had plans for us that went beyond the ring and that felt as intimate as it could get. More so than anything we had done before.

When I saw that the gym was empty, I checked Bobby's office to make sure he was gone as well and then I locked Levi and me in. I tossed the keys on the counter and made my way to where Levi had been working out for almost an hour. His endurance and continued strength impressed me. Most guys got tired quicker, but then again, Levi was muscular and cut without being overly so, therefore his muscles didn't tire out as quickly from the weight of them.

Rounding the corner of the ring, I stopped when I realized Levi had already stopped punching. He was pulling water from his bottle into his mouth, some falling down his body. His headphones were still in but he heard my approach because he glanced my way as I came to my stop.

I waited, unsure what I should do. He was a man I had spent a lot of time doing dirty things to, but was still shy when it came to something more between us. We fought and fucked, and as I stood there getting more and more anxious, I wanted that dynamic back more than I wanted anything.

After tossing his bottle to the ground, he used his forearm to wipe away the excess running down his face and started stalking toward me. I didn't want him to see how nervous I was, so I straightened my stance and crossed my arms.

"We alone?" he asked, gradually looking around.

"Yep," I replied, like it was just circumstantial.

He threw his gloves off fast, not bothering to look where they had landed. He took two steps toward me and scooped me into his arms, making me wrap my legs around his waist. I didn't want to, but the giggle that came out of me couldn't be helped. It was like a switch had gone off in him and everything was finally okay.

"I thought we were going to fight," I reminded him as he carried us into the men's locker room.

"We are, but not now and not here."

We walked straight into the showers and were immediately assaulted with cold water. At the same time, his mouth found mine and warmed me back up instantly.

While the water changed from cold to hot, we undressed one another, trying our hardest not to separate our lips. My legs wrapped back around him and he pushed me against the wall behind the water. We were aligned, and he thrust himself up to find his home inside my body.

"A week is too long, Charleigh. I'm becoming addicted and need more."

"Yes," I hissed, agreeing with him.

My affirmation made him thrust harder, and I held onto his shoulders for dear life. His mouth had moved to my ear, and I could hear his deep grunts as he fucked me. My pussy started pulsing and squeezing, coming like only Levi could make it do.

He followed behind me, kissing my neck and licking at the water that was splashing on me from the shower head. When he had finished emptying himself inside of me, he let me down gently and without saying anything else, he started bathing me. He even took a hand down and rubbed our cum from between my legs.

When we were both clean, he pulled me from the shower and kissed me again before demanding that I get dressed. I had to sneak to the other locker room, but it didn't take me any time to get back out to the main part of the gym where he was waiting on me.

He was dressed in fitted jeans and a t-shirt, the most casual I had ever seen him. Even in the joggers that he coached in, he didn't seem as casual as he did in jeans. His joggers were a uniform of sorts, something he wore for work. His suits were for interviews, meetings, and one-night stands.

His jeans were for a night out with me.

He threw his bag over his shoulders and walked toward me, taking my hand with a delicate squeeze. I was surprised when he kissed me, gently. So intimately that I swooned in a way I never thought possible.

What was he doing? What was happening?

We locked eyes as he brought my hand down, bearing witness to his effect on me. I may have been tough, strong, and ready for a fight, but I was also vulnerable and susceptible to falling for the charms of a man like Levi.

No, not *like* Levi... just Levi. In my head, I was supposed to hate, him but that was never true. I just hated that I couldn't have him. Although that didn't feel true either. I had him when I wanted him. Now, he was setting a new table for us, and I wanted to sit down and see what he had to serve.

In the back of my mind, I considered it to be a trick, something to get me to lower my guard. I also thought about how I was keeping a secret from him about his fight while he was busy making me feel like a queen. I flinched a little, knowing I should tell him the truth, but I also didn't owe him anything and Bobby everything. Levi had been nothing but trouble and rage since we reconnected on that football field all those weeks ago.

"Come on, Charleigh," Levi whispered. "Let me take you out."

I nodded, deciding to let all my worries and insecurities fade away for the night. I had let everything fade away when it came to Levi. I was already an idiot. My career was already in his hands. I had said yes to going out that night because I wanted to, and I still wanted to see it through.

We walked hand in hand to the door, and I let us out with the key. It was dark and always kind of scary on the streets at night, but I was used to it. Those were my streets. But I paid attention to Levi, hoping that Mr. Malloy, the homeless man who did drugs by the trash can after dark, didn't spook him.

"My car is out back," he guided me toward the turn in the

sidewalk that led to the back of the gym. "Let me put my bag up, and we will take the Marta."

"The underground train?" I asked, even though we all knew what the Marta was. I was just shocked he wanted to take it, especially when we both had cars parked in the parking lot.

"You okay with that?"

"Of course. Are you?"

He smiled as he popped his trunk open and threw his bag into the back. "I prefer it." Leaving his car probably wasn't his best move, either. There was a forty percent chance it wouldn't have wheels when we got back, but I kept my thoughts to myself and took his hand again.

He guided me down the block to the Marta station, passing Mr. Malloy quietly with a small nod. We got onto the train without talking much but I did note he was taking us to the center of the city, around Centennial Park.

"What's the plan, Coach?" When I called him coach, he looked around to make sure no one heard me, but I had already made sure our train was empty before I said it.

"Taking you somewhere special, somewhere I should have taken you long ago."

"I have to admit, I'm both intrigued and scared." Not just by where he was taking me but also by the fact that he was being so romantic while doing it. Our fingers were still interlocked, and his other arm was wrapped around me.

He nuzzled close to my ear and lowered his voice as he answered, "You should be."

levi

THAT WAS GOING to be the only night I had with Charleigh before I had to start pushing her off the field again. I had to get her to leave the NFL. That was all there was to it. The text from Richard a few days ago drove that home.

I was nuzzling my nose into her ear, soaking in her scent and the heat her body exuded when I was close to her. Darkness had settled in and for a Friday night, the train was empty. I had thoughts of laying her back on the bench and licking her pussy until she came. It was almost the only thing I could think of, especially since she sucked my dick so selflessly during the last game. I wanted to return that favor.

"Why should I be scared?" Her voice interrupted my memories.

I leaned back from her, hoping I could coherently answer her question. "Because, baby, it's still my mission to destroy you."

"So, this sweet side is just an act?" She smirked without looking at me.

"Yep." I leaned in and kissed her ear again, unsure if I was telling the truth or not. Was I being sweet? It felt like I was being selfish. I needed one night to stand down and then I was going back to being the guy I had to be. Was that an act?

"Where are we going again?"

"Almost to our stop."

She shook her head and smiled, not able to handle the surprise I had cooked up. Although it wasn't much of a surprise, and the closer we got, the more worried I was about my plans. How would she view it? What would it tell her about me?

The train began to slow close to Centennial Park–close to home. I wasn't taking her to my penthouse, even though it was tempting. Rhys had once again flown to Miami for a doctor's appointment, and the place was empty. I could spend hours, maybe even a whole night like when we were in New York, worshiping every inch of her. It would beat the hell out of the short quickies we'd been forced to sneak in. I just couldn't take that step, knowing what was waiting for us on the other side of the weekend.

I grabbed Charleigh's hand once again, praying it was late enough and dark enough not to be recognized by anyone as we passed through the center of the park. I didn't get recognized much, since the focus was always on the players, but sometimes people saw me and it clicked right away.

Looking up toward the building I lived in that sat next to the park, I told myself one more time that taking her up there was a bad idea. It was just a coincidence that I lived near where I wanted to take her, not a sign that I needed to divert from my plan. Leaving my car insured I had to go back to get it, and that helped me remember my plans.

"Okay. I'm confused." Charleigh leaned into my arm, holding me close as we continued to walk. "Most everything down here closes early. So, are we picnicking in the park?"

I pointed ahead to a small row of businesses. "We're going right over there."

She stayed silent but her eyes started darting around. There was no way for her to tell which direction we were going; everything was closed like she said, but she continued to look around, curious as ever.

When we got close enough, she stopped, right before we crossed the street from the park to the buildings and looked up.

"You are not serious right now," she mumbled before slowly turning her eyes toward me. The smile on my face was too big to hide the fact that I was dead serious. That if she assumed we were headed into the business in front of us then she was completely correct.

"Eye Solutions?" She threw her hands in the air and started turning in small circles, but I could hear the humor in her tone. "You really do want to fight with me, don't you?"

"I told you I would take you for glasses. I'm just living up to that promise."

She stopped her circles in front of me, face to face with her back to the buildings. "And what? Is there a doctor there waiting to test my eyes?"

"Maybe," I shrugged as I pushed my hands into the pockets of my jeans.

We stared at one another, each with a smirk on our faces, occasionally shaking our heads. I had a good plan, but unless I gave us something to fight about, it didn't feel like us. So, I took her to the guy who gave me my glasses–that I never wore unless I read a novel. He trusted me with the key to his business under the explanation that I wanted to use his rooftop access for a date.

That wasn't a lie. The roof was where we were headed, but to get there, we had to go through the office, and I fully intended to test her on the eye chart and fit her for some specks.

"Come on, let's find you some eyes, Ref." I turned her around and we crossed the road hand in hand. She waited while I unlocked the door and once inside, I flipped on a small light. Just enough so we could see, but not so much that everyone passing by would think the office was open. I locked the door behind us to ensure no one would come in, just in case.

I wrapped my hand around her waist and guided her to the eye chart, turning her as she stood on the line of tape on the floor for distance measurements. She was laughing at every turn, knowing I was teasing her and getting a kick out of the effort I was going to.

"Okay, Ref. Tell me what that first line is." I pointed to the biggest line of shapes and covered one of her eyes myself as I stood behind her.

"Elephant. Car. Football—"

"Beep," I cut her off. "That is not just a football, it's a first down, Ref."

Her laugh turned into a giggle, and I was starting to believe that the eye doctor had been my best idea ever. If I thought I loved her fight, it was nothing compared to the way her body shook and bounced in my arms as she laughed at how ridiculous I was.

"Let me try again, Coach."

With one hand on her waist, I reached around and covered one of her eyes again. "Go."

"An elephant the size of your ego. A car that I will run you over with. A ball shaped like the ones your wide receivers can't catch. And a pair of lips, that you can kiss my ass with."

"You think you're cute, don't you?"

"You started it," she chuckled as I turned her around to face her in my arms.

"You still got one wrong, though. My ego can get pretty large, but when you can make the sexiest referee in the league come in under five minutes, it goes without saying that it's going to inflate a man's ego."

"I will give you that, so what about the car?"

"If you want to run me over with a car half as much as I want to run you over with one, then fair is fair."

"And that means your wide receivers can catch?"

"No," I leaned in and pecked the tip of her nose. "They just have the best quarterback ever throwing them bullets, so the wide receivers are just lucky bastards."

"That means you have no intention of kissing my ass." Her eyes narrowed a little, humor laced with lust shining bright as we got closer and closer.

"No, Stripes, not today at least. But that pair of lips will be kissing your lips," I pecked her lips then moved down to her neck. "Your neck, your ear, your cheeks, your forehead…" I trailed off, kissing her everywhere I was telling her I was going to. Before I backed away, I added, "I'm going to do other things to your ass, though."

charleigh

I COULDN'T HAVE BEEN ANYMORE ATTRACTED to Levi than I was at that moment. He was saying all the right things, making me feel fun and free. Teasing me with a trip to the eye doctor was not only corny, but perfect. It showed me another side to him, one I had no idea was under all the mean and nasty words he normally spewed.

Our safe words.

The ones that kept a wall between us.

Words I spewed right back to him because I had to.

Would we go back to those two people? Or was that night the beginning of something else? More importantly, were we risking too much for something too weak? A physical attraction that wouldn't withstand the damage we would wreak on our careers in the process?

Enjoy tonight, Charleigh.

I let Levi lead me up the stairs in the back off the office area where snacks had been set up on the roof top. I gasp at the romanticism of it all, moving slowly in case there was a booby trap waiting to whisk me away.

"When did you do this?"

"I had my housekeeper drop some things off before Dr. Jay closed up for the night. I went to Bobby's to work out and just prayed it was all still in place when we got here."

The building wasn't a huge skyscraper, only two stories high. But it overlooked the park and in the distance were the bigger buildings of Atlanta, all lit up and glowing. It added to the ambiance, like huge night lights for us to gaze at while we ate.

I took a seat on a bench near the wall of the roof and waited as Levi poured us a glass of wine. When we were settled with a glass in our hands and snacks sitting between us, I realized I had a million questions I needed to ask.

Did I risk changing the moment because of my curiosity? Should I go ahead and tell him about the fight? I had questions for Levi before I betrayed Bobby. I needed to know I was telling someone who wouldn't stab me in the back in return. Levi may have been a true romantic that night. He may have been making me swoon and laugh. He was definitely making me feel special. But I would be an idiot not to keep my guard up. Enjoying the evening didn't mean I was dumb.

"Is this all still because I sucked your dick?" I cut my eyes at him playfully.

He shot his eyes back and smiled as his lips touched his wine glass. "Maybe."

I followed his sip of wine with one of my own, hoping it calmed my nerves. "Can I ask you something?"

Where did I start? Did I start with what his intentions were with romancing me when I was clearly always up for sex? Did I ask about what the deal with Richard Elder was? Or did I just skip straight to wondering if he would be mad if bets were placed on his rematch with Sisco?

I didn't get the chance to ask any of it because instead of letting me ask a question, he had one of his own. "What happened in Chicago?"

"Chicago?" His question took me off guard. I wasn't prepared for him to ask anything, much less about what happened in Chicago.

"After the game," he added, even though I knew exactly what he meant. I could also tell by his expression that he already knew the answer to that question as well.

"Nothing that I'm sure won't happen again." I tried shrugging off the conversation since it made me both sad and uncomfortable. It took a lot of pep talks with myself to get me to relax for the night, so I didn't want to start off with old shit.

"It better not," Levi demanded, making a statement that only I could hear, but felt like it was directed at everyone in the world.

"What do you care?"

"Torturing you is my job. Touching you is my job."

I flushed at the memory of Chicago and number sixty-seven coming up behind me. Instinctually, I swiped at my shoulders as the memory relayed itself. It was like I could feel him over my shoulder all over again.

"I saw what happened." His eyes were stern as mine seemed to widen with his words. "I watched the game footage and as everyone else watched the play, I watched you."

"Number sixty-seven," I confirmed. "Leaned over my shoulder like he was asking me something about the game and called me a cunt. I don't take too much offense to that word but if he was trying to get under my skin, it worked."

"Keep going," he urged, clearly wanting the whole picture, including the part he could see from the video.

I sighed because I knew I was going to tell him. I had nothing to lose anyway. He had already seen me in tears over it–my weakest moment. "He kept on like that the entire game, under the guise of talking about the game of course. He didn't fucking play, so he never left. And toward the end of the game, when he realized his words weren't cutting deep enough, he used his jacket to hide his hands and took a finger to the back of my ass."

Levi shoved to his feet and paced down the length of the rooftop, then back. When he made his way back in front of me, he leaned down and put his face in front of mine. "Keep going."

"There isn't much more to tell. I felt violated and hurt, emotional. My first season with my dream job and I get treated like that? Honestly, coming from you after a play isn't actually bad, it doesn't bother me at all. I expect that to be the case. But a random player who has no business even talking to me, much less touching me?" I shuddered again as Levi knelt down in front of me. "I want to be respected, and two games into the regular season I was sexually assaulted in front of millions of people."

"Why didn't you say something? Why didn't you at least tell *me* after the game?"

"What would you do or care? I knew why you were there, and I was okay with it. If anyone else saw it, it would be all over the news, so when it wasn't, I just let it go. I need to work on being someone before I can start whining."

Levi leaned in closer and took his hand to the side of my face. Gently, he took a few hairs that had fallen in my face and tucked them behind my ear. "Baby girl, I would have cared. I do care. I may give you a hard time on that field, but I do not condone anyone getting away with what he is getting away with."

"That is big, considering you have threatened me with your cock laid against me."

"I'm different, and you know damn well I am. I've never touched you on that field in front of millions of people, and I have never touched you without your consent."

I was starting to tear up at the truth behind his words. Every time his hands have been on me, even when we were fighting, I wanted it more than I wanted my next breath. That was the pull that started in New York and continued the moment I was in his world again.

I nodded at him, assuring him I agreed with what he said, then bit back the emotions. I had my own questions, and since he got one in, it was my turn to ask.

levi

I HAD RESETTLED on the bench next to Charleigh and bowed my head. I knew number sixty-seven touched her, I could see her jump in the video, but I wasn't sure how until she told me.

"I have a question, too. Remember?"

I looked at her and nodded, telling her to go on with her question.

"Are you and Mr. Elder playing me right now? Is this all a ruse to get me to quit?"

Oh fuck if she only knew. Quitting is what I wanted her to do. Richard wanted more than that from her.

"I'm not playing you right now," I said honestly. "I wanted a calm and honest night with you. I wanted to spend time with you outside of the ring and off the field. That's it."

"I just don't know what to believe."

"Yeah, you do." I sat up straight and leaned against the bench. I crossed my ankle over my knee and tried to look sure of myself. "You wouldn't be here if you thought I was playing you."

"Yeah, I would." Her answer was quick and matter of fact. "I don't feel like I have control of myself around you. My body isn't strong enough to back away from you even if you're using it to destroy me."

That was my chance to push her away and tell her she had to go. That I needed her off that field and off all the other fields. I could lie and tell her I would tell the world about us and destroy her reputation and career before it ever got started. Then, she could back away on her own terms, and I would win both battles.

Instead, I pulled her from the bench and sat her in my lap. Her left arm wrapped around my shoulders, and I leaned back so we could both see the buildings across the park. I pointed at a tall building, and her gaze traveled down my arm and into the distance.

"See that building right there? The one with the three flashing red lights?"

"Yeah," she said softly.

"I own the top floor. That is where I live. And I wanted to take you back there and recreate our night in New York. I want to push you against my huge windows and crack the door to the balcony a little so that I can show my neighbors in the other buildings who you belong to. Your tits pressed against the cold glass, you screaming my name so loud they can hear you through the small crack. I want you to call me Levi, not Brett, because when you say my real name, I know that you know exactly who is fucking you."

Her eyes were still staring at the building, even though my hand had lowered to her thigh. I let my thumb graze over her jean-clad pussy a few times, just enough to tease her as I spoke the way I did at the bar in New York.

"You want that, Charleigh? It's what we do best, isn't it? Fight and fuck? One more time, baby girl. Let's go see how high you can lift those legs, how hard you can get my dick, and how many times I can make you come."

Picking her up, I stood, turned her around, and set her on her feet. Grabbing her face, I leaned down and kissed her, then looked into her eyes while I waited for her to tell me to take her home with me. That wasn't my plan at all, but at that point, I was sure she thought it was always part of why I brought her there.

After what she just told me, I couldn't help myself. Just a few words about how much her body wanted me was enough to make me oblige. I was helpless, and on top of my need for her, I wanted her to stop questioning me.

"Why not just start with that?" she asked. "Why tell me you wanted a quiet, honest night with me?"

"I'm not planning any of this, baby. Just going with what feels right."

Her hands started caressing up my chest until they were around my neck. "That is all I have ever done when it comes to you. Whatever feels right. Throwing that flag in your face a few weeks ago felt right. Fucking you in my locker room felt right. Being here tonight feels right. But it's dangerous, not only to my sanity but to my job, livelihood, and heart."

I flinched at her saying I was dangerous to her heart. I didn't want her heart, nor did I want to be a risk to it. And I sure as fuck didn't want her to be anywhere near my own heart. But I would be lying if I said mine didn't stutter a little at her words.

"Let's go, Coach. Let's go spend time together the way we do it best."

A growl rose up inside of me and I kissed her as it escaped my lips. She let out another one of her small giggles that I had become addicted to and wrapped her arms around my shoulders. Our kiss lasted a few minutes, basking in the feeling and taste of each other, reminding me of when I was younger and the act of kissing was enough to turn me on.

Now, not only was it turning me on, but it was also satisfying me in a way it never had before. Like I could finish the night with nothing more than that kiss and still be happy and content.

When the kiss ended, we quickly gathered the food into the

bag and finished our wine before heading out across the park once again, this time in the direction of my building.

Our hands were laced and our smiles were almost puckish. We both took sweet and subtle glances at each other as we made our way through the dark park. I had the bag of food on my shoulder, knowing without a doubt we would need sustenance after a while, and my apartment was bare since Rhys had left.

It was late, but not past midnight and for a Friday night in Atlanta, some still considered the time early. Plenty of people were roaming the sidewalks, so I kept my head tilted down, as did Charleigh. Neither of us wanted to be recognized and chose to be safe rather than sorry.

Once we made it into the lobby of my building, I felt even more uneasy since more people there knew who I was and may recognize Charleigh as my date. Luckily, the lobby was empty, so I strode quickly toward the elevator bank and pressed the up button. My penthouse required a key for the elevator, so I dug into my wallet while we waited for it to come down and open.

I kissed Charleigh's temple on instinct, just needing the contact. I was just about to wrap my arm around her when the door to the elevator opened and the couple about to exit was none other than Tyson Black and his girlfriend, Giselle Metrovik.

They were kissing, and so far into one another that they didn't see me yet, but I knew they would. So, without thinking it through, I shoved Charleigh quickly, making her fall between the two large imitation bushes that sat along the elevator.

"Coach!" I heard Ty say happily. Then he looked toward the bushes, realizing I had just been looking at them. Charleigh couldn't be seen, so he asked, "Like the greenery, Coach?"

"Um, what?" I asked, worried I had hurt Charleigh and not paying enough attention to what he had said. When it registered, though, I nodded. "Weird that it's here in the building like that. But I just realized it was fake. Giselle, how are you?"

Giselle nodded and let me change the subject. "Good, Mr. Peyton. Just taking it day by day."

"Where are you two headed so late?" I was clearly nervous, just wanting them to leave, but also knowing I was throwing red flags right and left by being so jittery.

"Ice cream," Ty smiled. "Trying to convince Miss Priss here to live a little. Coach? Is that a purse?" Ty motioned to my cooler that sat on my shoulder, much like a woman wore her purse.

"Uh, no, it's..." I couldn't tell him it was a picnic cooler. I would fall right out of my hard-core, tough reputation and into a laughing stock quicker than I could say 'good game.' I patted the bag a few times, trying to decide what to say before genius hit me. "It's my gym bag."

Ty nodded with his lip jutted up and I knew without a doubt he didn't believe me. He had seen my gym bag a thousand times. It had the Jets' logo on the side of it and looked more like a bag used for the gym. This cooler looked almost dainty.

Fuck.

"Hope you had a good workout, Mr. Peyton." Giselle smiled and winked at me gracefully, and I nodded a silent thank you. She may not have realized I just shoved the new NFL referee into the fake bushes, but she knew I needed to be spared the scrutiny of Ty's hard stare.

"Sure did. See you tomorrow, Ty. Flight leaves at 2 pm."

"Aye, aye, Coach." He gave me a salute but stayed put for a few more seconds.

My phone chimed and I grabbed it, seeing a text from Charleigh on the screen.

This is war.

Ty is standing right here. What did you want me to do?

NOT fucking push me.

You love it when I push you.

I smiled at my text, forgetting I had an audience until I heard Ty clear his throat. "Okay Coach, have a good night, I think."

I took the goofy smile off my face, replaced it with my famous scowl, and nodded. I hit the elevator button to tell them I was going up and thankfully, that did the trick. They turned and headed out the door and because there were glass windows around the entire lobby, I waited a few more minutes before I reached for Charleigh.

Stay put until I grab you.

I think I broke my ankle, you idiot.

charleigh

I SAT behind the bushes that Levi pushed me into with my arms crossed over my chest. I get why he did it, and if I was being honest, I was thankful he did. I didn't want to be outed any more than he did–probably more. But damn him for thinking I was Sisco's size.

A bruise was going to form on my shoulder, and I really felt like I had twisted my ankle, although I may have exaggerated the pain in my text. It definitely wasn't broken, and I probably could have walked out of there if I wanted to.

When his hands parted the bushes and his head poked through, a look of concern flitted all over his face. He held his hands out and I reached for them, his eyes staying on my ankles.

"You didn't break your ankles," he noted, relieved.

"No." I let him pull me up and back through the gap in the bushes. "But I still may kill you. And you're still an idiot."

"But Tyson Black has no idea you're here, so be mad, but take it out on me upstairs."

The elevator doors reopened and luckily, no one was in there. We rushed in and willed the doors to close quickly as Levi swiped his access key to the penthouse.

"I forgot Ty's girlfriend lived in my building," Levi said as he leaned against the rail.

"How could you forget that?"

"I only had one thing on my brain, and it wasn't Ty or his girlfriend." His gaze darkened, the moody coach he normally was returning to his features.

I had no response to the way he focused on me. It was intimidating, and aside from how he wore jeans instead of a suit, it was reminiscent of how we took the elevator up in New York. The same jitters of excitement hit every nerve in my body, and I had to grab the rail behind me to keep from falling to my knees for him.

When the elevator made it to the top floor, we were welcomed into a private foyer, not overly gaudy but with all the finer things that made a penthouse a penthouse. He walked me to the only set of double doors and entered a code, making the door unlock and open for us.

"After you, Stripes." Levi motioned for me to go in first and I did, expecting to be bombarded with all things luxury and over the top. To my surprise, the foyer was no indication of what I found inside his home.

The windows were huge, floor-to-ceiling, and wrapped around the exterior walls of the entire penthouse. I imagined every room that had an exterior wall was windows, but other than the obvious God-like feeling of being on top of Atlanta, everything else was understated.

His leather couch looked worn down, a few years old, and incredibly comfortable. His decor was mostly random football memorabilia and a few pictures of a woman I assumed was his mom. There were shoes scattered by the door, a jacket thrown over a chair, and when I looked to the right, into the open concept kitchen, I saw dishes sitting in the sink.

It made him human, a man I could relate to because while he did live in the penthouse, his home wasn't pretentious. It reminded me of my home–messy comfort–and since I didn't spend a lot of time at home, a wave of contentment washed over me.

I walked farther into the main room, suddenly feeling like I was where I was supposed to be. I wasted no time removing my clothes and tossing them on the chair where the jacket was strewn–a single item at a time. I knew Levi was still by the front door, watching me as I made myself at home. But he didn't move until I was completely naked and turned around to face him.

He pushed from the door where he had been leaning and watching, making his way to me like a predator. The bag of food he had been carrying was long gone, tossed onto the pile of shoes I saw when I first walked in. His strides were long, and as he approached, he shed his own clothes, not bothering to put them on the chair but opting to leave a trail as he walked my way.

Without knowing why, I backed up a little, making him walk further to get to me, but eventually, my back hit the coolness of the window.

"That is right where I wanted you," he smirked, shedding his jeans and showing me how hard he was. His cock was thick, pulsing as he eyed me, and I licked my lips, thinking of how hot it made me when I wrapped my mouth around him. "Touch yourself," He added as he stroked his cock. "Show me how you pleasure yourself when I'm not around."

I slid my hand down my stomach and opened my folds, allowing my fingers to access the wetness that had already started dripping from my body. I pulled the moisture to my clit and started rubbing, watching as Levi's eyes took in my motions.

"Ever since New York," he started, "I'm the only thing you think of to get yourself off, aren't I?"

I nodded even though he knew the answer.

"Baby, my dick doesn't even work for anyone else but you. I've tried so hard to fuck your memory away, but my dick only wants you."

I nodded again, agreeing with him that my pussy only showed any interest when he was around or when I thought about him. That was why it was so messed up, so hard to turn away. That was why no matter how wrong it was, I allowed myself to open up for him. I was being controlled by something stronger than my brain. I told him he was a danger to my heart, and I meant it. My heart was now controlling my body.

Levi and I didn't do a lot of talking when we were together, and definitely never too deep. Keeping things on the surface and calling it a fight was how we rationalized our disobedience to our jobs, but those walls were falling faster than the penalty flag I threw at his feet all those weeks ago.

Not only did I want him to fuck me and make me scream, but then I wanted to fall into his couch and ask him why he had so many shoes by the door, who the woman was in the pictures, and if I could see one of his Super Bowl rings.

I had to let that all go, so I pressed harder to my clit, knowing he was watching and wanting to connect to him the only way we would allow ourselves to do. I moaned, and my knees started to get weak as I got myself closer and closer.

The view of him stroking himself in front of me–in front of the world–was erotic. I was pressed with my back to the window, aware of the small lights that were on and allowing anyone with a view, access to our private moment. It was a small taste and a huge risk that anyone could see Coach Peyton and the new NFL referee were sexually entangled.

And the idea of being caught was freeing.

After a few more strokes to our own bodies, Levi closed the gap and spun me around, pressing my tits to the glass. He placed my hands above my head and my cheek pressed into the window, keeping me steady as he pulled my ass up.

"Oh fuck, Ref. Every time I'm behind you on the field, I think about pulling this ass to me. I think about how under those black, straight pants are curves that make me weak. Sometimes, I even think about bending you over, right there in front of all one-hundred thousand fans and showing them who you belong to."

I moaned at the thought, and I knew I would never be able to be on that field again without the image of what he just described.

"When you throw the flag, I want to spank your ass and fuck you until you tell me you got the call wrong. I think about it every single time. The way your mouth closes around the whistle makes me wish it was my dick, lucky ass whistle."

While he spoke, his fingers roamed my body, squeezed and caressed every part of me he deemed necessary for his attention. When he lined himself up to me, I moaned once again, unable to form any words. I just wanted him to fuck me. To make the vision of us on the field feel real, even though I knew it would ruin me forever.

"Ready, baby?" he whispered.

"Yessss," I managed to get out. "Please."

"Say it, Charleigh. Tell me to fuck you."

His thumb started to press onto my tight, back hole, making my eyes widen, and words even harder to form.

"Tell me to fuck you," he demanded again.

My chest started to heave with nerves as he continued to touch me where no one else ever had. It felt salacious, crude, and so good I wanted to cry for more.

"One day I will," he said as if reading my mind. "But right now, tell me to fuck you." He punctuated each word with a grit of his teeth and a nudge of his dick to my opening.

"Fuck me," I finally cried. "Fuck me hard, Coach."

He barely let me finish before he thrust into me. He knew I liked it hard, and he wasted no time burying himself as deep as he could. In and out with a force so strong my tits and cheek started to ache against the window. Still, I begged for more.

"Harder, harder."

Levi growled, giving me what I asked for. Pain and pleasure started to overlap, pleasure winning out as I got closer and closer to coming. Right when I thought I was about to let myself go over the edge, Levi pulled out and dragged me away from the wall.

Using his hand in my hair, he bent me over the couch and drove back into me. He moved his hands to my hips, keeping me in place as he continued fucking me hard. He brought me back to the edge, getting me close to coming again and I was ready for it, wanting it more than anything.

But once again, he pulled out of me, stopping before I could find my release. "Fuck you!" I yelled because he knew what he was doing. He was bringing me so close to the edge and denying me the euphoria. He knew I could come a hundred times by his hands–or dick–but he wasn't wanting that. He wanted me to suffer.

"Oh baby, I'll let you come. I swear I will. But when you do, I want you squeezing and convulsing on my dick so hard that I feel the same pain you do."

Picking me up, he walked around the couch and sat down, my legs straddling his lap. He lifted me and lined himself up to me before forcing me down hard. Then he let me take control. I moved my pelvis, my thighs, and ass as I ground on him fervently.

In no time, I was close again, but that time, I was looking into his eyes. His mouth teased my nipples, his teeth taking small nips. I watched him play with me and watch me like he was studying my face to learn what made me feel the intoxication he wanted me to feel.

Face to face was intimate, and even though it wasn't the first time we fucked like that, it seemed to be more than we had ever given to each other.

I held tightly onto his shoulders and moved, my heart connecting to him in a way I knew I needed to run from. His head fell forward and he rested his forehead between my breasts. I gently traced my fingers up his shoulders until my hands were in his hair, caressing and tugging so he knew I saw and felt him.

"I'm gonna come," I whispered. "So hard I squeeze you out of me, just like you want, Levi. So, you better hold on tight."

I sped up, and he lifted his head, refocusing back on the forceful fucking he was doing before. He pushed his hips upward and met me halfway as I fell onto him over and over again.

Then I was staggering with an orgasm so strong I was sure I would end up on the floor, blacked out and unconscious. But Levi was there, holding me as I let go and following me over the edge. His head threw back against the couch, his mouth open, his breaths short, and a small noise escaping with each one.

We rode the high together, and when we came down, our eyes reconnected. We sat there staring at each other, taking a mental step over another hypothetical line we shouldn't have crossed.

levi

WE ENDED up in robes on my balcony, eating the snacks from the bag and finishing the wine we had started before we changed the course of the night. We were both fully aware that once we were fed, we would head right back to fucking one another and would do so as long as we had the time and energy.

For the time being, though, I was happy just having her the way I had intended in the first place when the night began. We found ourselves talking without yelling, discussing things without questions of our debauchery or intent.

"I had no idea you grew up on the streets in Oakland," she smiled, popping a grape into her mouth. "I guess I thought you were always just rich and famous."

I barked a laugh. I had told her about the pictures of my mom and how she still lived in Oakland and did work with kids who didn't have safe places to live. I had told no one about my upbringing before, but it turned out we had a lot in common.

Single moms.

Younger brothers.

Poor childhoods.

Finding our consolation from our love of football.

She told me about her brother and why she worked at Bobby's, while I told her how I ended up at Al's, needing a place to let out the anger I sometimes let fester inside of me. But we quickly steered clear of the rematch I had agreed to, Charleigh not wanting to talk about it for some reason.

All she told me was that she thought it was dumb and that I should back out. She also said she had asked for that day off, and that the only fight she wanted to see was the Grishom and Holt fight that was in a few weeks.

A money fight.

Pro.

Vegas.

Not the quiet, small gym fights we were doing. But I had been fighting that kind of fight my entire life. They were all I had outside of the game of football that I did solely for myself.

I didn't expect her to understand, so I changed the subject to something that wouldn't start a fight. I learned a lot about her own path to the NFL, and I saw how much it meant to her to be a part of the game. I just wished it was easier said than done, because she had no idea the depths the owners stooped to for the almighty dollar. She was nothing but a pawn, and the best thing for her to do would be to leave altogether.

After a little conversation, I pulled her back into my lap and opened her robe, tasting her nipples as they peaked under my touch. Her hands ran through my hair, and we were once again set off into the oblivion we created when we were together. Nothing else mattered and there were no consequences.

I wished it could last forever.

But by four in the morning, and with so much sex that neither of us was going to be able to walk, I reluctantly let her get dressed and drove her back to the gym. I had already had someone get my car, so I drove another car I kept in the parking garage.

We kissed outside in the parking lot until six, and the sun was threatening to peak before I watched her drive away safely in her own car.

I managed four hours of sleep before I had to be at the practice complex to ride the bus to the airport. Instead of my usual planning and obsessing session on the flight, I slept the entire time, raising the suspicions of my fellow coaches on whether I was feeling sick or not.

Ty eyed me a few times as well, but never said anything other than a nod and a quick, "Good to see you, Coach." He was letting me off the hook for the night before because the more I thought about it, the more obvious it was that I had been spending time with someone that I didn't want him to know about.

He still wouldn't have known it was Charleigh Wright, though.

By that evening, I was settled into my room, on my bed, and I pulled my phone out to call Charleigh. It was foolish, but I dialed anyway, and when she answered, my smile stretched so wide my face hurt.

"Hey, Coach." Her voice sounded like she was smiling, too.

"Hey Stripes," I used the nickname some players and coaches called the officials. One I had called her a few times. "You naked?"

Her laughter warmed me, and I tucked my free arm behind my head, settling in for what I hoped was a long talk with her. "You're ridiculous."

"I completely agree. So, tell me, did you sleep the day away?"

"Oh, hell yeah, I did. No traveling for me. No game to officiate. No work to do at Bobby's. Mom and Jesse were at the flea market all day. So yes, I slept, cleaned, relaxed, and read a book."

"Sounds like heaven. I fell asleep on the plane, so now everyone around me thinks I have the flu."

She laughed again and then asked the million-dollar question. "Why are you calling me, Levi?"

"I don't know, Charleigh. I just felt like it. But I do have a question."

"Okay..." she trailed off nervously. "Shoot."

"Not this Monday, but the next, I have to fight Sisco. So, for every moment I am not coaching, Al wants me to be getting work in at the gym. The old man cleared his schedule, and I kind of feel like I owe it to him to put the time in."

"Or you could cancel the fight," she suggested again.

She had been insistent that it was dumb and silly. That Sisco was just butt hurt and I didn't have to prove anything with a rematch. That she was over the whole fighting scene and probably wouldn't even be there. Bobby had asked her to call the fight, and she said no.

But none of that was why I was fighting. I was doing it because I wanted to. Because it was fun and freeing. Something I had done for myself for as long as I could remember. It didn't matter what she said, or how foolhardy she thought it was, I was fighting. But I wasn't going to fight with *her*. Not when we had finally found solid ground to exist on together.

"Okay, we won't talk about the fight, but my point is that I have a full schedule next week and probably won't see you until the home game next Sunday."

"So what? Another quickie at halftime?"

She was keeping our relationship about sex and fighting, just like we said we would do, but for some reason, I grimaced as she spoke. "No Stripes, just warning you I will be full of agitation and insults by then."

"And pent-up sexual frustration, I'm assuming. Since you have been getting some pretty regularly these days."

"Think you can handle it?" I teased.

"Bring it on," she countered. "I could use a good fight, and you're my favorite coach to throw the flags at."

My laugh was a bark, surprised by her readiness to go head-to-head next Sunday during the game. The day after that would be the fight and since she had no plans on being there, whatever we said on the field would have to fuel me for the spar the next day. I needed her worst, or her best, however you wanted to look at it. Nothing made me want to hit someone more than Charleigh being on that football field.

"Rest up this week, baby, you're gonna need it," I teased.

"You too, Coach."

I hung up on that note, knowing I couldn't drag out an intimate conversation with her. It had to stop there. But then I had an idea, a deal I could offer her. And even though I was making the deal in jest, a part of me hoped she took it.

Pulling my text messages up, I found her name and made my plea.

If you quit officiating, I will cancel the fight.

I smiled when I sent it, picturing her rolling her eyes as she read it.

Fuck you, Brett.

Ouch, okay maybe not.

charleigh

I TOSSED my phone across the bed, annoyed at Levi's text. Just when I thought I might betray Bobby for him and warn him about the fight, he reminded me of how much he wanted me to fail, and I no longer cared if he was outed in the ring.

Maybe if Richard found out about his boxing hobby, he would pick on him and leave me alone. So, fuck him and his fight. Fuck his need to see me run off the football field. And fuck the way our night at his place made me feel. It was all nothing but complications and distractions.

Mistakes.

I would see him Sunday, and everything would be back to normal as I called my best game and he bitched behind me about how much I needed glasses.

In the meantime, I was going to enjoy my week. Having the weekend off always rejuvenated me, and I was looking forward to the work I had planned at Bobby's all week, mostly because I was taking Jesse with me a few days so he could get a workout in himself.

On a whim, I took my phone and blocked Levi's number, not wanting to risk him messaging me anymore and ruining the good mood I knew I would have all week. Then I called my mom and planned a shopping date for good measure. Even though I hated shopping, it made her happy to browse and spend time with me. Making her happy made me happy.

I was already getting my Levi-free week off to a great start.

I was right–my week was bliss.

Simple.

Like old times.

Lots of family time, me time, and time at the gym with the people who cared about me most in the world.

Then Sunday came around, and my high fell to my toes. It wasn't that I didn't want to officiate the game, but more about fighting off the feelings I had for a man who wanted my demise to be imminent and messy. It didn't matter how good he was at making me come. His chauvinistic attitude was the biggest red flag I had ever seen.

Still, I sought him out when I made my way onto the field. I met with the crew and we exchanged small talk as the teams warmed up around us. I couldn't find Levi, but I kept searching, getting more and more obvious about my intention as time went on.

Finally, I saw him standing back behind a crowd of people watching warmups. He was in his normal stance of concentration–legs wide, arms crossed, one hand to his bottom lip, tugging as he watched.

I turned back to my crew before he caught me and tried to shake how sexy he looked out of my vision. There was something else about how he looked, but I couldn't place my finger on it.

And I sure as hell wasn't going to do a double-take and figure it out.

Somehow, I managed to get through the entire pregame without looking back at him again. But when I started making my way down to my locker room to collect myself before the game, I spotted him off to the side in the corridor. He was animated, angry, and telling someone all the things he wasn't going to do.

Whoever he was talking to was slightly hidden behind a wall. If I ventured too far out to see who it was, they would have been able to see me, so I stayed close to the edge of the corridor and tried to hear whatever I could.

It wasn't much, though. Levi was saying, "I won't..." and the sound would trail off. Then I would hear, "I can't..." and the rest was indiscernible. His arms threw into the air and he turned around to stomp off, but with another quick thought, he turned back around.

When he did, he saw me, standing there with my eyes wide like I had been caught doing something wrong. But I was exactly where I was supposed to be.

Instead of looking away sheepishly, I just raised one eyebrow at him as if to say, "*What*?" I didn't hear anything but who cares if I had? He should have had his argument somewhere more private. He was the one having the animated conversation where everyone could hear.

With me staring at him, he chose not to say whatever he was turning around to say and walked off toward the locker rooms. I stepped out a few steps to see who he was arguing with, but they were gone.

I rolled my eyes at how nosey I was and headed to my locker room. Whatever Levi had going on that week shouldn't have bothered me. He was a man with a lot of stress and anger, so I shouldn't have even been shocked he found someone else to fight with.

A splash of water to my face, a drink, and a quick change of my socks–for good measure–later, and I opened my door to head back out to the field for the coin toss.

But I gasped when I took my first step, immediately stopped by Richard Elder standing against the wall outside of my door and away from where everyone could see him.

"Can I help you?" I asked politely, not wanting him to see my disdain for him so bluntly.

"Just wanted to check on you." He smiled, but it held an air of phoniness. Richard gave me more red flags than Levi ever did, but he held his closer to his chest. He said ominous things that meant nothing to me but somehow gave me chills.

"All good. Game time." I closed my door and walked past him, but he grabbed my arm by the bicep and stopped me.

"I expect you to be thankful you are here, Ms. Wright."

I pulled my arm from his grasp and leaned back, finally seeing him for the cold man I knew he was. "Excuse me?"

"Coach Peyton has been nicer than I will be."

With that, he walked off, strutting toward the field like he hadn't just thrown me into a tailspin. What the hell did that even mean?

Did he know about Levi and me?

Was that what Levi had been doing with me? *Being nice?*

I needed to get to the bottom of it all, I just didn't know how or where to start. At that moment, though, I needed to call a good game and do my job. As long as I did that, it didn't matter what Mr. Elder's warnings meant because I would be doing the job I was paid to do–correctly.

When I returned to the field, I shook my arms to loosen the tension that had built up. I kept my head down, checked in with the officiating crew one more time, then took my position with kick-off minutes away.

As I stood with my hands on my hips, I could feel the moment

Levi made his way behind me. He wasn't right up on me, but he might as well have been because I felt like I could feel his breath on my neck. My body was imagining his warmth against my back, and I turned my head subtly side to side to get rid of the thought.

I thought he would leave me alone, stand back, and let the game start. But as we waited for the ball to be set on the field for kick-off, he made his way to my side.

He had his arms crossed over his chest, his headset around his neck, and if anyone was watching–which they for sure were–we looked like we were just discussing the game. I wished we were discussing the game.

But the game seemed to be the last thing on his mind.

levi

"YOU BLOCKED ME," I said flatly.

I was annoyed, angry, and maybe even a little hurt. We had had such a good night before I left, and even though we weren't supposed to be getting closer to each other, I felt like we had–and it felt good.

When I called her after the game last Sunday, I expected her to tease me about throwing the red flag with the same attitude she had thrown the yellow one at me. I thought maybe I could ask her about a call made by the acting line judge, and she could give me her take since I hadn't seen the film on it yet.

I was looking forward to smiling with her, teasing her, and even asking her what she was wearing just so I could imagine her rolling her eyes at me one more time. Was I in too deep? You better fucking believe it. But it was unstoppable, and after all the anger and stress I carried around, I didn't have it in me to fight with her anymore.

But then I realized she blocked my number.

The only good thing that came out of that was the fact that the hits I got in with Al were the strongest I had ever had. It ate at me all week and I let it out the best way I knew how. I was ready for my fight with Sisco the next day, he didn't stand a chance, but I still wanted to know if she was going to be there or not.

"I had to, Coach."

We stood side by side, as if we were discussing the weather, and kept our eyes on the field. I had turned my headset off so no one could hear us and with all the lip readers out there, I lowered my head a little when I spoke to her.

"Why?" *Fuck, I sounded like a kid.*

"You know why. But thank you for being *nice* about it. Mr. Elder assured me you were the good cop."

I lost my aloof appearance, whipping my head around and yelling, "What did you just say?"

"Not here, Coach," she gritted out as she put her whistle in between her lips.

"Yes, here. Right the fuck now. Did he say something else to you?"

Dave crowded around me and asked me if everything was okay, and that was all it took to remind me I was on the field and had to coach. I backed away, letting Dave pull me to my side of the line as the kick-off signaled the start of the game.

"What the hell was that about?" Dave asked as I readjusted my headset over my ears.

"Nothing," I seethed.

It was bad enough Richard had approached me right before the game with his bullshit, but the fact that he dared to speak to Charleigh again made me want to strangle him.

I looked around the sidelines really quick, seeing if he was still on the field or if he had made his way to his suite to watch the game. When I didn't see him, I turned to glance toward his private box. Even though he was so far away in the stadium, I hoped he was looking down and could see the hate I had on my face toward him.

"Coach?" Cam had come up beside me and I turned around,

giving my quarterback my full attention. The guys playing on the team, the ones I cared about most in my line of work, were the only reason I didn't leave the field and march up to Richard right then and there.

"Yeah?" I glanced up at him as he was slightly taller than me, though not by much.

"Last year, I risked my career, public scrutiny, and even my freedom because I fell in love."

His words seemed to be coming out of the blue. I didn't understand where he was coming from or why he was saying them. I just lowered my headset again and furrowed my eyebrows at him in question.

"It was all worth it," he added before patting my back and running onto the field for our turn on offense.

Thank God for Cam because he served as a backup head coach, calling plays and arranging the offense while I stood there dumbfounded. It was anger I felt, not love. I wanted to don my hardest-hitting gloves and cause bruises. Not because I was in love, but because I was in hate… with Richard Elder.

The whistles blew and pulled me from my daydreams about breaking my knuckles on my boss's face, and I checked back into my job.

Charleigh was waving her arms, signaling to the head referee what call she was making so he could announce it to the crowd. Then she turned to make her way back to the side of the field.

We locked eyes and she stopped walking, seeing something in me that even I wasn't aware I was conveying. I wanted to reach my hand out to her, pull her to me, and have her tell me everything that was going on in that gorgeous head of hers. Then I wanted to fix it for her, no matter the cost.

It would be worth it.

Cam's words came back to me as the thought of risking my career to make sure she was okay scrolled through my mind.

It was all worth it.

I turned my back to Charleigh, allowing us both to take a breath and get back to work. Eye to eye, face to face, we only saw each other. And even though I started the day off pissed that she blocked me, I knew that if Richard was also feeding her bullshit, she had done the right thing to block me and save herself from the possibility that I was involved.

She had seen me talking to Richard before the game. He was telling me I needed to control her, intimidate her, and make sure she knew who to thank for her career. I told him no. I had been telling him no.

But what did she hear? What did she assume we were talking about?

I tugged at my hair, wanting to leave the field and take her with me. How was I going to wait the entire game to talk to her, to make sure she knew that despite my eagerness to get her off the field, it was never because I didn't believe in her or want her to succeed, but it was always to protect her from the owners, like Richard, who saw her as nothing but a means to more money, clout, and someone they thought they could intimidate into controlling?

Charleigh wore her dreams coming true on her sleeve. The entire world knew how important it was to her to be a referee in the NFL, and I knew from the moment I met with everyone in New York that the new female referee would be exploited and utilized in a manner that no other referee had to deal with.

I didn't want that for her, no matter who she ended up being. But once I found out it was the woman I couldn't stop thinking about from New York, I became even more enraged. I'd wanted to save, spare, and extricate her from the dirty side of the game that no one else ever saw. I wanted to do all of that, while still saving myself, my job, and my livelihood.

But I don't think I cared anymore. The truth had to come out, even if it cost me everything I had worked so hard for. Charleigh deserved to know why I was insisting she leave, but more importantly, she deserved to have someone stand up for her and what she was going through and shed light on gender inequality in the NFL.

They wanted the praise of being on the right side of history, the approval of public opinion, but that wasn't the reality of the movement for Charleigh. She just didn't know it yet. I never wanted to hurt her feelings, or to make it known to her what was really happening. I just did the dumb thing and pushed her too, hoping that if she left on her own, the joke would be on them.

I was going to tell her after the game. Screw the media, the interviews, and even my post-game speech to the team. I was going to go straight to her and give her everything she deserved to know,

After several minutes of reflecting, I zoned back into the game and tried to be the best coach I could while I could. Because after I betrayed Richard, and the NFL, I was sure I would be out of a job.

Thankfully, the resolve in my heart made it easier to focus, and the game started flying by. I even threw in a few obscenities at Charleigh for calls she probably nailed but I still didn't like.

Halftime, I left her alone, knowing if I saw her our conversation would start too soon and have to end before it was settled. But by the end of the third quarter, I walked up beside her during a timeout and told her what I needed from her.

"I need to talk to you after the game. It's important."

"I'm not having sex with you," she said with her head down to hide her lips.

"We already know that if I insisted, then you would open your legs for me, baby." Okay, so I had to throw that in for the sake of being us.

She huffed a small laugh and shook her head in annoyance.

"Really, Charleigh. Please hang around and let me explain some things to you."

"Fine," she agreed but with a clip in her tone.

I took it though and walked away before she could change her mind.

Unfortunately, the next play on the field ensured I never got that chance.

charleigh

WHEN MY EYES connected with Levi's on the field, I knew I was done for. Not once had I been able to deny him with my body, but now I felt my heart being tugged more and more, and I had no defense mechanism to save it.

The look in his eyes told me he was just as shook as I was about Richard talking to me the way he had, and now he wasn't even able to coach the game. Behind me, the entire game, I heard the assistant coach and Cam Nichols plotting and planning the plays.

Levi was quiet and every once in a while, I heard someone ask if he was okay. It made me melt little by little to know he was warring with himself the same way I had been. By the time he told me he wanted to talk, I was too curious and needed to know what he had to say.

I tuned back into the game after the other team's timeout was over. I settled in on the ten-yard line, as the Jets were in the red zone and close to scoring.

Everything was heightened on the end of the fields because everyone played with extra pep and power when they got that close to scoring. I knew I had to be extra alert and focused.

It was Atlanta's ball and Cam Nichols took the snap, jumping back a few yards to give his receivers a chance to run their routes. I went down the line, making sure I was properly placed for a call that was most likely headed to my side of the field. Ty Black got directly in front of me and when I saw he was wide open, I knew the ball was headed toward him.

But so did everyone else.

Ty caught the ball and turned to run, but the defense caught up to the play and pushed him hard, forcing him out of bounds. With me standing behind him, I was shoved as well, and was no match for the size and strength of Ty's body.

He slammed into me hard, and I went backward several steps before I lost my balance and started to fall violently to the ground. I braced myself with my arms, hoping I could spare my head from hitting the ground, but it all happened so fast.

Within seconds, I was down, and a whirlwind of people were crowding me, asking if I was okay. I tried to focus, but there was so much commotion and concern. The voices were coming from above me; all I wanted to do was shove them and tell them to move.

I anticipated the pain, but it had yet to come, which I first thought was the adrenaline. But then I felt a small caress across my face, a familiar voice, and my blood warming from the comfort of the arms I was in.

"Charleigh," Levi whispered. "I got you, baby."

It was so low, no one else could hear. He spoke directly into my ear while everyone else was shouting. But after comforting me for a few seconds, he looked up and shouted at everyone. "Back up, give her room."

The crowd began to back up and I was left with Levi and the team physician, who leaned in and started asking me questions.

"Did you hit your head, Ref?"

"No, I don't think so," I shook my head, trying to sit up.

"Stay put, ma'am. Just until I can evaluate you."

I rested back, wanting to curl into Levi's arms where I felt safe from prying eyes.

"I got you," he reassured me. Then I could hear him speaking to the physician. "I caught her before her head hit. She should be okay."

"You okay, Coach?" the physician asked.

"I'm fine. Worry about her."

The physician helped me lean up and Levi steadied me as he and I both stood. I looked around and realized with him always positioning himself so close behind me, he was there to catch me when I fell. With all the equipment and people around, I could have been seriously hurt. but thanks to him, I was fine.

It was my natural inclination to step toward him and hug him, but I fought the urge after a half-step in his direction. I wobbled, but only because I caught myself about to make a very public mistake–with a million pairs of eyes watching.

The physician grabbed me as I put my foot back down and then pointed toward the bench nearby. "Sit down. I'm going to request you be evaluated as a precaution."

"No, I'm fine."

"I trust you, Ms. Wright, but let's be safe."

The head referee had made his way over and crouched down as I took a seat. "We can cover the rest of the game. Make sure you're good."

"Yes sir," I agreed.

The game resumed, and I was escorted toward the corridor. I glanced around to look for Levi and caught him standing in his usual stance, giving me a quick nod, before turning back to the game.

When I made it to the physician's office beside the locker rooms, he gave me a quick evaluation before deciding he wanted to ensure I didn't have a concussion.

"I need to send you to the hospital for a quick CT."

"No," I shook my head. I knew I hadn't hit my head, so it was pointless. And if I left, I wouldn't get to talk to Levi.

"Ms. Wright. I'm insisting, but I promise it will not take long. Without one, they may make you sit out two weeks so I think if we just have the proof that you don't have a concussion, then we will be a step ahead."

I laughed at the way he said *we*, like getting the scans was a team effort. When in reality, I was sent with an uptight escort and dropped off at the hospital with CT orders, where I sat alone for four hours.

By the time I called for a cab to go home, showered, and shoved a frozen meal down my throat, I was exhausted and fell straight into my bed. The emotions of the day, along with the soreness from being pushed, lulled me straight to sleep.

I was being chased by a defensive safety for a football team that didn't actually exist. The guy was huge and scary, though, and I was running as fast as I could. Sweat was dripping down my face and I was reaching out, trying to get to the end of our tunnel. At the end of the tunnel was Levi, begging me to hurry and cheering me on as I got closer and closer.

I woke up with a start, my head coming off the pillow so fast I was dizzy. I had to look around to remember where I was and even what day it was.

Leaning back on the pillow, I smiled at how silly my dream was–like some warped reenactment of what had happened at the game, minus Ty being there. Levi was trying to save me, just like he had been when he caught me and kept my body from slamming into the ground.

I sat up once again, panicked, because I had just remembered that the game was the day before.

Which meant it was now Monday.

The day I was supposed to go to my other job.

But I settled back down, remembering I had called in ahead of time for that day off. That I already knew I didn't want to be there. It was the day of the fight, and I wasn't sure I was going to be able to see Levi...

I sat up once again, only that time, I didn't stop. I ran from my bed and to the living room, searching for my phone while simultaneously trying to find the clock I had on the wall and hoping the time was correct on it. I spent so little time at home that I never bothered to change my clocks.

When I dug my phone out of the bottom of the bag, I was shocked to see I had no calls and only a few texts from my mom asking me to check in and enjoy my day off. None from Bobby, none from Bond nor Axton.

None from Levi.

It was if my brain had fallen into such a lull that it was returning to me in stages and only as needed. Because I remembered I blocked Levi, and he wanted to talk after the game, and I wanted to listen. I had also told myself I was going to tell him about the fight because even if he was teaming up with Richard to make my life hell, he was failing and making my life full.

I didn't want him to fight.

I didn't want him to go in blind.

I didn't want him to show up and have everyone recognize him.

I looked at the time and realized the fight was supposed to start in an hour, so I ran to my room and got dressed while at the same time unblocking Levi's number in my phone.

I pressed CALL on his name over and over again, voicemail picking up each time. I had no idea what time he was going to get to the gym, but I knew he would be oblivious to Bobby's show until he walked into the doors. Bobby had already ensured everyone who was attending was to be there well before fight time and no cars were allowed in the lot.

Levi was going to be blindsided and before he would be able to back out the door, everyone would have already seen him come in.

Dressed in ripped jeans and a tank top, I grabbed my keys and ran for my car. Bobby's was only fifteen minutes from home and I told myself I would make it in ten.

I just hoped it was fast enough.

levi

"I'M NOT GONNA LIE. I'm so glad you're here."

"I don't like to miss your potential ass beatings," Rhys said around a mouth full of the apple he was eating. The apple reminded me of Charleigh, but I had been trying to squash her out of my thoughts until after the fight.

It killed me that I never got to talk to her. She was long gone before the game ended, and with my number still blocked on her phone, I had no way to check in on her. I didn't even know where she lived.

I came close to canceling the fight altogether and spending my off day hunting her down, but I knew my best chance to find her would be to start at Bobby's. She said she wouldn't, but maybe she would end up showing up after all.

Rhys was driving and turned the blinker on to turn down the road toward Bobby's Gym. "You think you are showing up a tad too early?"

I shrugged because I imagined I was a bit early. But if Charleigh were there, it would be worth it. If not, I could just sit around in the locker room until Sisco was ready to rumble.

Al was on his way, but he was unprepared for me wanting to

go earlier than necessary. I assured him I would be okay until he got there. I didn't need a babysitter, just my brother to help me not run off with Charleigh. Not that he knew about her yet. But he knew someone had gotten to me and he was on what he called "Levi watch" for a good old-fashioned freak out.

When he flew in late Sunday, and let himself into my apartment, I breathed a sigh of relief I hadn't known was festering. He didn't ask about it, just distracted me, and I was thankful for him knowing what I needed.

Rhys pulled around to the back of Bobby's and together, we made our way around the front and to the sidewalk. My bag was slung over my shoulder and my head was down. I was trying to focus and get into fight mode, but a lot had changed since the last time I fought Sisco, and my heart wasn't as into as I thought it would be.

I settled my hand on the door and took a deep breath, giving myself one last chance to walk away. The only thing keeping me there though, was the hope that Charleigh was inside waiting for me. So, I pulled the door open and led the way into the lobby.

Instantly, I knew something was wrong.

There were too many people, too much heat.

Rhys walked in behind me and all I could hear was him saying, "Holy fuck," over and over again. He pulled me back, but I resisted, too stunned to move.

Bobby started in my direction, a smile of satisfaction all over his face.

"We'll cut you in," he laughed, like that was my main problem.

I started shaking my head and licking my teeth, anger getting deeper and deeper into my bones. Everything was elaborate, and there was no way Charleigh didn't know. She had to have known about that plan for weeks and never once told me.

That stung worse than the fact that everyone was about to see me, and possibly recognize me. I had seen Al do the same thing at his gym, hoping the opposing fighter got rattled and he was able to make a pay day. It was underhanded, but in their world, it was what it was.

Bobby didn't know I was Levi Peyton, he thought I was Brett–a regular guy that wanted to fight. Sisco didn't know either. But Charleigh did, and she could have stopped this.

I felt a push on my back, only it wasn't Rhys. It was softer, warmer, and definitely not strong enough to move me. I looked backward and down, right into Charleigh's eyes. They were huge, sad, and apologetic, leaving me torn between relief at seeing her, and anger at her not being honest with me from the start. She knew who I was, and the risks involved with me fighting.

She didn't care.

And I guess I couldn't blame her.

But at that moment, I couldn't stand to look at her. Because now that I was there, I had to fight. I couldn't back out. My options no longer existed.

Rhys was telling me we should leave, but my ego was telling me to take out the rage out on Sisco and show Bobby why I was the wrong one to place bets against. His surprise audience didn't rattle me the way he had hoped it would.

Charleigh pushed me again and that time I gave a little, letting her guide me across the lobby. Bobby started to follow but the door opened again, and it was Al. His face went into shock when he saw the crowd mingling near the ring, and he looked to me and then to Rhys.

Al didn't know who Charleigh was either, so he was extra confused as to why she was trying to push me away.

"Bobby, you talk to Al, I need to talk to L... Br... him." Charleigh grabbed my arm and pulled me into the office, shutting the door for us to have privacy.

The door opened back up immediately, and we both whipped

around to see Rhys poking his head in. "Can you tell me who knows what and who? I am going to fuck this up."

"Just tell Al it's all good and to get ready for a fight."

He hesitated, but then nodded and shut the door back.

Charleigh spun back around to face me, her head shaking as she tried to find words. "You can't fight."

"I can fight, Apple." I leaned in so she knew I was angry before adding, "It's your day off, leave."

"I tried to call you. I have been dialing for thirty minutes. I tried beating you here. I tried to warn you."

"You could have warned me weeks ago. You could have never blocked my number and chose to tell me any time last week," I shouted. "But you chose not to and that's fine. It's better this way. Just more proof that I am doing the right thing."

"The right thing about what? Richard is going to have a cow."

"Richard has bigger issues, and we can deal with those later. I need to go get ready."

"NO!" she screamed again. "Please don't fight."

I paused before I passed her to get to the door and looked down at her slowly. "Is the fight rigged?"

Her eyes squinted and her nose snarled. "Bobby would never..."

I didn't let her finish, just pushed past her and opened the door again.

"Let's do this," I nodded to Rhys and Al, who both thought I would run. "I'm ready to hit something."

"No... please..." Charleigh cried behind me.

I didn't look at her, but I paused and listened to her breathing for a minute. Then I walked past everyone and to the locker room, Rhys on my heels.

When I sat down on the bench, I pushed my hands through my hair and tried to suppress a scream. Every instinct I had told me to go to her and give her what she wanted. But she didn't yet understand that the repercussions of the fight no longer mattered. I could explain that later, but I had a lot to sort through first.

And I couldn't do it before I taught Bobby and Sisco a small lesson.

"Okay, so I have pieced most of this together, but do you need to get it off your chest before you fight?"

I looked up in question. "Pieced *what* together?"

"The hot ref," he motioned toward the door as if Charleigh was standing there. "She also works here for Bobby. You two are in love. Shit is about to hit the fan. You're gonna fight because you know you will be fired anyway once the league finds out about your relationship. All that."

"Is it that obvious?" I smirked, almost humored at his take on it.

"Yeah bro, it is. But if you are gonna fight, then get it off your chest first."

"I'll worry about Charleigh later," I sighed. "I'm still a little pissed she didn't tell me about this shit show."

"Oh, I'm sure she had a good reason," he laughed, indicating he knew more than I thought he did. Were we that transparent?

I nodded, agreeing with his statement but not wanting to add to it. I needed to get into fight mode. Charleigh needed to be my fuel. All I would have to do was look her way and be reminded of how much anger I had inside. Poor Sisco was going to get the wrath of her transgressions.

When it was time, Bobby made the announcement that the fight was starting and introduced me as 'Brett.' I pounded out of the locker room to a round of boos, making me laugh a little inside at the small-time fanfare. Being that I got booed by hundreds of thousands of people during every away game, their disdain for me didn't even hit my scale of discomfort.

My eyes were scouring the room, looking for the woman who made me want to fight everything and everyone–including her.

The woman who I was so mad at, yet still so enamored by. The woman who made my heart race, but somehow calmed me at the same time.

"She left," Al said into my ear when he saddled up beside me.

I stopped looking around, trying not to show my hand to anyone else. Al and Bobby probably didn't know the story, but they knew she and I had *something,* considering how hard she was trying to get me to leave.

From then on out, I let her go. My head was in the fight, in the motions, and in the hits I knew Sisco was going to get in. I had prepared for that moment, needed it, and craved it. It was finally time to let myself loose.

I shed my shirt and the fight started quickly. Sisco had been working out hard because he was stronger and faster. He was more prepared and landing tricks that I hadn't seen before.

By the final round, I knew I was up. Despite how hard Sisco had worked, I wanted it more. I always wanted it more. I didn't make it to the pros as a football player and then become the youngest coach in the league because I half assed my desire to win. And the one thing I wanted most in my entire life was to always win.

Not just the fight, but in life.

Sisco had hardships I could never relate to, but he was young. One day he was going to get a fight like this, or maybe even on a larger scale, and he was going to beat the shit out of his opponent and prove his greatness.

But that wasn't going to start with me.

charleigh

COULDN'T STICK AROUND and watch. The guilt was eating away at me so deeply that I felt physically ill.

Al and Bobby were going to want to know what the hell was going on, but I could answer their questions later. Fight day, with all those people around, was the last place we needed to have that conversation.

Not to mention, I wanted to talk to Levi first. I no longer wanted to risk mistakes where he was concerned.

After the game the day before, the way his eyes told me I was okay and that he was there for me, I knew I should have been more honest with him. Even if he hadn't been honest with me, he told me he wanted to talk, but I never got the chance to hear the secrets I knew he needed to divest.

Then I was too late getting to him.

Too late to tell my own secrets.

The look of anger and confusion he gave me would forever stick with me. At that moment, he didn't look like a grown man, he looked like a hurt and lost boy.

I went straight to my mom's, not wanting to go home and be alone. After the last couple of days, I needed her and the comfort that only Mom could bring me. I also needed to talk to her and tell her the truth.

As if sensing her daughter's emotional distress, she threw the door open before I could let myself in and wrapped her arms around me. It never ceased to amaze me that I was thirty-five years old, and she still had a hold on me like I was a child.

"Baby girl," she said, smashing her face to my cheek. "You okay?"

"No," I said flatly.

"Let's go inside. Jesse is playing video games so we can have girl talk and some lunch."

I followed her in and sat at the table in the kitchen, waiting quietly as she prepared sandwiches. Not until she sat down and rested her hands on her chin did I finally spill my guts.

"I think I'm in love with Levi Peyton."

Whatever she was expecting me to say, that wasn't it. Her eyes shot wide and she drew herself back in her chair, needing to create enough space to think.

"The coach?" she finally asked. "The one who spends most of his time yelling at you on the sidelines?"

"Yep." I nodded, and took a bite of my sandwich. Even I was in shock by what I was saying, but it also felt good to finally be honest with myself.

"Like, real love? Or a crush?"

"Like real love, Mom. The kind that makes me obsess over him in a way that I swore I would never do with a man. The kind that makes me make mistakes, take risks, and then run away. I have spent the entire season so far wishing he was someone else so I was free to be with him. But even our positions with the NFL haven't stopped us. Even when I thought he may be my demise and kill my career intentionally, I still sought him out and let him find me when he wanted to be near me."

I went on to tell her how we met in New York, how he showed

up to fight Sisco, and how we had only had one night together that didn't involve us fighting. I told her that I didn't know what to do with my new job, or what kind of future I had if the truth ever came out. I also confessed that I had already considered quitting, like Levi had insisted I do from the beginning.

"Did it ever occur to you that he wanted you to leave because he felt the same way about you and knew he couldn't pursue you if you were employed by the NFL?" Mom and I were done eating and her shock had turned into motherly concern.

I tilted my head back and forth, mulling over what she had just said. Was it possible that Levi wanted me to quit because he loved me? Was that even the right thing to do?

"I think he wanted me out of his way. I think he knew we were too risky for our careers."

"So, it would seem he was right." It was more of a statement than a question.

"Yeah, I guess so. But I never considered being the one to leave. I worked too hard for that job."

"What do you want more? Him or the job?"

I laughed, loud and almost manic at that question because the truth was what hurt the most. "Doesn't matter. I won't get Levi, and after this season, I'll be traveling all over for games like regular officials, so I won't even have to see him as much. I just have to get through the rest of this year and then it will be like none of this ever happened."

"If you're in love, it won't be that easy," Mom reminded me. "You have to at least talk to him."

"I have two weeks until the next game. By then, I'll have built a defensive front around my heart."

While I was at mom's, I left my phone in the car, so when I got back in to drive home, I saw the twelve missed calls and forty-seven text messages from the guys at the gym. No one was specific, they just said to call ASAP. Axton and Bond were the main ones, but there were a couple of calls from Bobby as well.

My heart immediately went to my throat, worry coursing through me the way all my other feelings did. I called Bond back first, not brave enough yet to talk to Bobby after the show I caused with Levi before the fight, but Bond didn't answer.

Next, I tried Axton, but his phone also went to voicemail.

Something bad happened, I could feel it. I somehow managed to drive home but was unable to get out of my car from how sick I felt.

After a few minutes, I got the courage to call Bobby and as if he was waiting on the call, he answered quickly. "You okay, Kid?"

"Yeah, just had lunch with mom and forgot my phone in the car," I explained.

"I just wanted you to know Sisco beat the shit out of your boyfriend." His voice was calm, like he hadn't just ripped me apart with his words.

"Is he okay?"

"He walked to the ambulance, if that's what you mean." Bobby sounded as if he was talking about the weather. Like he didn't have a care in the world. He should have been happy Sisco won, mad that I hadn't been honest with him about Levi, or maybe even sad that he put in all that work for me to end up begging him not to even fight.

"The ambulance?" I swallowed.

"We called one as a precaution, but he seemed to be okay." A sigh of relief escaped me, and Bobby snorted on the other end of the phone. "You let me arrange a fight knowing that he was Levi Peyton."

"You had already planned the crowd and the bets before I even had a chance to tell you," I explained, like I was a little girl and Bobby was in charge of my punishment.

"I do that all the time, Charleigh. But I would have never intentionally outed a fighter who wanted to remain anonymous. That isn't my style."

I rolled my eyes because Bobby was only upset that the fighter was famous. Had it been any joe-blow from the streets, he wouldn't have cared about how that fighter felt about it. He always relied on the payout being enough to smooth things over. Levi didn't care about the money Bobby offered him after the fight, I could guarantee that. More than anything, Bobby was probably embarrassed.

"It was never my place to tell anyone, anything. I never told Levi about your plans, either."

"But you wanted to, didn't you? You came barreling in here earlier wanting to save him."

"He and I have enough on our plates on the field, adding more drama because of the fight seemed like too much."

"Well, I'll let you two work that out, then," he sighed. "I just wanted to tell you one thing. And you are the only person that I am telling this to, you got me?"

"Okayyy." *Great, more secrets.*

"Peyton blew the fight. He had Sisco so far down that in a vote, he would have won. Sisco was barely holding on. He allowed Sisco one good hit and when I say he allowed it, he dropped his defense and let it happen."

My jaw was open, and I was shaking my head. Levi wouldn't do that, would he?

I whispered the word, "No."

It was all I could manage.

"I didn't confront him, Charleigh. But I know what he did. I've been around the game way too much to believe otherwise. Then when I tried paying him out for the fight, he told me to give it to Sisco or toward something in the gym. Charleigh, he let Sisco win, and not even Sisco realizes it. I don't know why he did it, but I thought you may want to know."

"Thanks," I whispered and started to hang up, too dumbfounded to speak anymore.

"Oh hey, Charleigh?" I brought the phone back to my ear so I could hear whatever Bobby needed to say. "I know you wanted a couple days off, but I need you here tomorrow at six pm. We are having a staff meeting."

"Why?"

"Because thanks to this little stunt, I want to change some things around here."

I nodded even though he couldn't see me. I felt so guilty about the role I played that if he wanted to discuss changes, who was I to deny him?

I hung up the phone and started to call Levi, but I stopped. Calling him would only be torture. I was curious if he threw the fight, but not enough to risk anymore of my sanity.

Like I told my mom, I could take the two weeks off until the next game and fortify myself. Then it wouldn't matter what he had to say, I would be able to walk away with my head held high.

Not to mention, he knew I had unblocked him. If he wanted to talk to me, he could have called me just as easily. He was still angry, and that was good. Anger was easier for us to deal with.

As head coach and referee, we could have our next fight on the field, where it belonged.

levi

I HAD sweat dripping down my body, my gloves on my hands, and a hat backwards on my head. I was moving to the beat of the music that was playing, watching my footwork and coordination. It didn't matter the song, a beat was a beat and even though I didn't dance, footwork always got better by following a beat.

The music wasn't too loud, so I could easily hear the approaching footsteps that made their way toward me as I took a few last punches at the air.

"What are you doing here?" Charleigh asked, leaning on the side of the ring in the middle of Bobby's gym.

"Waiting on you." I crouched down and got as close to her eye level as I could. I leaned on the ropes and squinted my eyes at her, still angry at her for almost everything about her since I had met her.

"Was this a set up?"

I shrugged because it was and I didn't want to admit it. Before I left in the ambulance to be checked out from Sisco's hit, I told Bobby to give my earnings to the gym and to make sure Charleigh was ringside the next day. I wasn't wasting another second before she and I laid things on the line.

"Get in the ring," I demanded. Bobby had done me a huge favor and made sure the gym was empty. It was just Charleigh and me, and we were about to have our biggest fight yet.

"Why?" she asked without moving.

"Get in the ring," I said again, standing up and tossing some gloves at her that I had brought with me. I backed away to the other side of the ring and leaned on the rope at the opposite side, crossing my arms and waiting for her to do what I said.

It took her a minute, but I had no problem waiting and watching. She was in long leggings, a sports bra, and one of those tank tops that hung low enough to see her bare waist on the sides. She took a hair tie from her wrist and put her hair up into a high ponytail, then climbed slowly under the rope.

Picking up the gloves, she slid them on and pounded her fists together. She started jumping from side to side, warming up and getting ready for whatever I threw at her.

"You fucking lied to me," I said without moving.

"And you fucking lied to me. At least I feel bad about it."

"When did I lie to you?" I shouted, unable to control the emotion she brought out in me.

"Everyday!"

"About what? Because I told you to get off the field? I didn't lie to you. I was very honest about what I wanted you to do. Or maybe because you think I have been working you over with Richard? Sorry, baby, I wasn't doing that either. So, tell me when I lied."

"What is the end game for you, Levi? Tell me the truth! You want to control me? Blackmail me? Have my career in the palm of your hands?"

I couldn't listen to that bullshit. She knew better than that. I pushed from the ropes and got in her face in the center of the ring, taking my gloved hand and shoving her enough to make her rock on her feet. "You know damn well that was never what this was about. You saw the shock on my face when I saw you on that field. None of this was my doing."

"I don't know what to believe."

"Yes, you do, but you need something to ease your guilty conscience for not being honest with me."

"That's not fair," she shouted, shoving me the way I had her. "Do you not realize the mind fuck I have been in since I landed this fucking job? Richard in my ear telling me he's watching me and implying that he owns me. You fucking me hard enough to make me forget about it all. Not to mention the other shit I deal with..."

"You've been a participant in the fucking, Charleigh. That wasn't just me. We both know there hasn't been a damn thing we could do to stop that train. It left the station in New York, and we never stood a chance after that."

"And as true as that is, Levi... I still never knew what to trust." Her face was red, and she had backed into her own corner of the ring, trying to stave off emotions as we continued to yell at one another.

"Come hit me," I demanded. "Come fucking hit me. I gave you those gloves for a reason."

She shook her head, denying herself even though I knew she wanted to let it all out. We were a lot alike in that regard. The force and power of throwing our fists helped us let the tension out.

"Get over here now!" I yelled. "You hit me, and I will tell you what you don't know yet."

That offer got her charging back to the middle of the ring, her right fist reared back and coming toward my stomach. I let her land the punch, feeling the sting from her strength even though she was far too small to ever hurt me.

"Richard was in New York with me." She was huffing from the exertion of her punch but listening with her eyes wide. "After we agreed to be a host to a new female referee, Richard cornered me and told me that this was our chance to own you–or whoever was hired."

She started shaking her head, her face getting redder from anger, so I pushed on before she combusted. "I never agreed. I told him I had enough on my plate and extortion wasn't on my list of things I cared to stress over. I was angry and almost quit my job and sold him out to the league before I ever left New York." I started pacing, angry at myself for not doing just that. "But that night, as I mulled over a glass of whiskey about how money hungry Richard had gotten, and how I would most likely lose my job if we didn't win another Super Bowl, I looked up from my drink and saw you."

I turned back to her and shoved her again, catching her off guard but knowing I didn't hurt her. "You!" I yelled. "I lost track of my anger at Richard and dove into my immediate connection with you. I let my dick run the night and instead of doing what I should have been doing, I was fucking a stranger in my hotel room all night. By the time I woke up, and you were gone, I had to catch my flight and all thoughts of talking to Art were out the door."

"So, it's my fault?" she yelled, and even though it wasn't, I raised my brows and let her think it was. "You're an idiot."

"I got back to work, and Richard laid off the idea until the week before that first game, when he told me the new referee was about to learn how 'little girls' didn't belong in the NFL."

She punched me again, and I welcomed it. "I belong there. I know just as much about the game as you do. I have worked my ass off to be there and I deserve better than to be thought of as a little fucking girl."

"I agree," I huffed as I let her get in another punch to my gut. "But I was in a fight for my career and even though I wasn't going along with whatever Richard had planned, I was lost inside my head being a coach, and not being your babysitter."

"But you did go along with it!" Her yells were echoing off the walls of the gym. "You told me every chance you got to leave."

"Richard didn't want you to leave, he wanted to extort you and control you. I wanted you to leave to save you from the chauvinistic and dirty side of the game. I wanted you to leave because you deserved better, and if you left, Richard wouldn't win. He is one of the richest and most powerful men in the country, trust me, you quitting was the only way he was going to lose."

"But you never told me that..." she seethed. "A lie by omission is still a lie."

"All I have wanted to do, from the moment you turned around on that field and looked me in the eye, was to protect you. I wanted you as far away from the corruption as possible, and I still want that. I don't regret what I have done and said to you, and until you are safe from the snakes and leeches, I will continue to be your biggest pain in the ass."

"Why can't you just be my biggest supporter?"

"Trust me. You won't win against Richard. I won't win against Richard. I have seen him bury more shit than I care to admit. So, I am supporting you, the only way I know how. But you also have to remember that I owe everything to my team. I vowed to be their coach, to guide them, and help them. Some of those guys, like Tyson Black, don't have anyone else in their corner but me. I know all too well what that feels like, and I had to make sure I could continue being there for them. I'm not sure Ty would have made it through the past few weeks if I had been fired, or quit."

Understanding was seeping into her eyes. The fight was leaving her as I watched her shoulders slump and her head dip down. She knew how important those guys were to me, and she knew I was trying my darndest to be everything to everyone. She took a few deep breaths and then looked back up at me. "What about everything else?"

"What else is there?"

"Us..." she flinched at her words, like they somehow made her feel desperate and weak. But to me, they only made me want her more.

"Everything between us was just us... it still is. It was never a part of any ruse to bring you down. I just couldn't help but want you."

She kept her eyes on me and I watched as they glassed up from unshed tears. Then without another word, she turned and started to leave the ring.

"Hold on," I called with my tone back to its demanding level. "We aren't done, Apple. It's your turn."

charleigh

I THOUGHT I was going for a staff meeting and ended up alone in the ring with Levi. I needed to remember to kick Bobby's ass because it had only been one day and that wasn't nearly enough time to shake Levi from my system.

As I listened to his story, about everything that had happened, I was both relieved and saddened. Did Richard own the world? Was Levi a coward? So much so that he would rather me leave my dream job than to stand up for me and demand respect?

I got that it wasn't that easy and that he had a lot of his own stress, but wasn't it worth something to him to be on the right side of a moral dilemma? There was nothing I wanted more than to leave him in that ring, alone, and to hide away until I could decide what to do with my own future.

"It's your turn," he said as I walked away. He used the term Apple when he spoke to me. He knew what he was doing, because that name reminded me of who I was the night I met him.

"My turn for what?" I spun around to ask him.

"Now tell me your truth?"

"Truthfully?" I charged toward him again. "I never knew what the fuck was going on, and you know it. I didn't care what happened to you because I didn't even know if I could trust you."

"Same for me," he shouted. "Why risk our jobs when we don't even know the other's intentions, right?"

I was directly in his face, wanting to punch him again just to feel the satisfaction. "Is that how you validate being a coward?"

"I'm not a coward!" he yelled. "I'm just a selfish asshole who did exactly what you did–tried to save myself."

"Well then, we have nothing left to explain. It's not like we even owe it to each other. It's not like there was anything more than sex between us. So, let's just let it go. I'll see you Sunday, Coach."

"Is that why you came running in here, begging me not to fight?" he asked before I could try retreating again.

"I was trying to do the right thing, that's all."

"Why? Because we're having sex?"

"No because…" I started to say that I cared about him. But we passed that window and I didn't want to reopen it.

"You and I both know this isn't just sex, and it never fucking was. We can fight it until we are blue in the face, but you and I were going to end up here from the moment fate brought us back together."

"I just want to hate you. Fighting you is easier than loving you."

I said it, so low I hoped he didn't hear me, but it was out there and I couldn't take it back.

"But loving you is worth the fight," he added, moving closer to me and reaching for my waist with his gloved hand. "This has never been about what we feel for one another, it's always been about what we aren't supposed to be to each other because of who we are. All my anger stemmed from not being able to have you, then to wanting more from you, then to protecting you, then to realizing I had dug a hole so deep and all I wanted to do was to be buried in that hole with you despite the consequences."

I leaned into him as his words were finally calm and settling my wild heartbeat. "Yet, nothing has changed."

"I fought yesterday because everything changed, so fighting didn't matter anymore."

"Why did you throw the fight?" I asked at the reminder of the fight.

"How do you know I threw it?"

I backed up a little so I could look into his eyes. Our gloved hands were holding each other but I wanted to see him when he told me. "Bobby knew."

He sighed in defeat, lowering his head a little. "I have no idea why I threw it, Charleigh. It just felt right. I was killing Sisco and before the last round, I looked across the ring and saw myself–a young guy who grew up in a rough neighborhood. Only Sisco hadn't been lucky enough to get out of trouble. He needed the payday, but more than that, he needed a win in his life. All I cared about was getting back to you, to find you, and fix whatever we may have still had. So, I let him get a hit in, and fuck it hurt."

I laughed for the first time since I walked into the gym that evening, picturing Sisco swinging on Levi. "Is that why you gave him the money as well?"

"I don't need it. I just wanted to get to you. I also knew Bobby would be more amiable if Sisco got the win."

"Bobby was angry I let someone famous get outed in his gym," I rolled my eyes. "He probably would have agreed to anything to make it up to you."

"Well, it turned out well for all of us then."

"This can't work out well for us, though. We're still a conflict of interest, Levi."

He pulled me into a hug and rested his gloves at the small of my back. "I have that figured out too, I just need you to trust me."

"But I don't," I reminded him.

"You have to start now."

I nodded against his chest, not willing to try walking away from him again. In a roundabout way, we both confessed that we were falling in love with one another. It was scary, but also a relief to know I wasn't the only one.

"How's your head?" He rubbed his glove over the back of my head while asking me about the CT scan we never got to discuss.

"Good. You kept me from hitting too hard. How's yours?"

"Good. Sisco hits hard but I didn't get up to let him get another one in."

"You up for one more fight, then?" I suggested, pulling back and shoving his stomach with my gloved hands.

"I will always fight with you," he smirked, pounding his gloves together and jumping from side to side.

I made a show of loosening my shoulders and stretching my neck. When I looked back at him, he was licking his lips and taunting me to come at him. I raised my fists up and closed the gap between us once again, that time swinging and trying to land punches.

He blocked everything I threw at him, never being shocked by the choice of moves or swings I took.

"Harder," he taunted me, urging me to push myself more.

"Aagghh ," I grunted, swinging again with my right arm before trying to fake him with a left uppercut. He saw it coming, not letting any piece of my gloves land on his body. That kind of fighting sense was how he was so good at boxing. He was not only strong, but strategic and could predict what the opponent would do before they did it.

I had one move he had never seen before, though. I just needed a minute to prepare myself for it, so I backed away and used my footwork to keep me loose.

When it was time, I lunged forward and jumped, wrapping my

legs around his waist and grabbing his neck with my arms. He wrapped his arms around me, and we found ourselves in a tight embrace in the middle of the ring.

Since there were no windows in the gym, we only had the dim light that shone above the ring. The music that had been playing when I walked in was soft, and we started swaying back and forth.

"This is a good tactic, Stripes. But if you ever use it on anyone else, I will spank your ass."

I groaned as his voice lowered back into that angry tone of his–deep and guttural. It had a direct line to my pussy, and I started throbbing instantly as I pictured him bending me over. I was hanging on to him like a monkey, grinding myself on his stomach, desperate to be with him again since it had been so long.

"Are we done fighting?" He pushed me down his body, just enough so I could feel how hard he was.

I unwrapped my legs and stood, but kept a hold of him. My mouth was near his ear, and I couldn't help confessing, "I'm scared."

"No, you're not." He took his gloves to each side of my face and held me tightly so he could look into my eyes. "You are one tough woman. Headstrong, smart, athletic, and independent. You turn me on just knowing that you can handle my bullshit. The way you throw insults back at me on that field made me start falling for you before I even realized what was happening."

"I can handle being tough, but being weak has never been my thing. A ceasefire with you is scary."

"Don't worry, baby." I could hear the smile in his voice but was still wrapped up in his arms so I couldn't see him. "We still have Sundays."

I laughed, but we only had Sundays until one of us got fired, or quit. How long would that be?

Before I could think about it too long, Levi pulled me away

from his body and turned me around. "Put your hands on the rope."

I did as instructed and then looked over my shoulder at him. He was eyeing my body, the way my ass was poking out at him, and the way my legs were slightly spread open. I watched him take his mouth to his gloves and start unwrapping them until they fell to the mat.

Then his eyes came up to mine and he smiled. "Leave the gloves on."

I nodded once, letting him know I understood and remembered how he liked it. But he also told me as long as the gloves were on, he could pretend it was a fight, and we were no longer fighting.

So, I leaned up and ripped my own gloves off, intentionally defying his request. I made up for it by removing my shirt and bra as well. He didn't even flinch, just smiled like he understood my intent. I placed my hands back down on the ropes and turned around so I couldn't see him.

He could do his best, but it was going to be without the gloves.

"Come home with me."

"Don't make me wait that long," I begged.

"I want you all night... all week."

"And now," I demanded.

"And now," he confirmed.

He held onto my waist and ground his hard cock between my cheeks over the top of my leggings. Then he started peeling them down, slowly, taking my panties with them. Then he took my shoes off and before I knew it, I was completely naked and his cock was nudging me from behind, teasing my entrance.

"Fast and hard." That was the only warning I had before he pushed himself inside of me. I nodded in agreement. Fast and hard. It had been over a week since we had been together and after all that had happened since, it felt like a lifetime. We needed the physical connection just to be able to think again.

Levi started milking himself in and out of me, hard like he promised but not as hard as he knew I liked it. I tried using the rope to help me push back into him, but he held my hips too tight, controlling the pace to his liking.

"Oh, Coach," I moaned. It turned me on to call him Coach, knowing how wrong it was that he was fucking the line judge for his next game. "Promise me at the next game, when you're standing behind me on the field, that you think about us like this."

He snorted. "I have all season so far. I have to yell at you just to keep my dick from showing the world what you do to me."

"Yelling at me has never tamed your dick." I moaned the words the best I could as he kept his rhythm inside of me.

"You're right." He took a hand and spanked my ass cheek, taking me by surprise and making me scream out into the echoing walls of the gym. "Nothing about you keeps me from getting hard."

"I stay wet for you, Coach," I gritted out. "Fuck me harder."

levi

"FUCK ME HARDER."

Her dirty mouth was making me insane. Every time she called me Coach, her pussy squeezed my dick and I had to slow down just to keep from spilling into her before I was ready.

I spanked her again, letting her know without words that she needed to watch herself. I would turn her ass red before I let it end. Fast and hard was the plan, but that didn't mean I wasn't going to savor it.

She took one hand off the rope, and I started to tell her to stop fucking around. But then she reached between her legs and took her nails to my thigh, leaving scratch marks that only she and I would know existed. The pain made me force my hips into her harder, but it faded quickly, as I realized she was trying to reach for my balls that slapped between us on every thrust.

It became a game as I went harder and faster to keep her from getting what she wanted. Eventually, she gave up and grabbed onto the rope again. She needed it to brace herself because I could feel her pussy getting ready to squeeze my dick to the point of madness.

"Fate brought you back to me," I confessed in the middle of

our ecstasy. "After New York, even the Gods knew there was no one else who fit me the way you do."

I pulled out of her, wanting to see her face when she came. So, I turned her around and pushed her into the corner of the ring. I lifted one of her legs onto the middle rope to keep her open for me and her arms held on to top ropes like they did the first time we fucked in that ring.

The sight of her posted up for me, completely naked, and her face so fucking alluring almost had me falling to my knees to worship her. She was the strongest woman I had ever met, yet let herself be vulnerable for me.

Just me.

"No one else will ever see you like this. No one else will ever get the chance."

I climbed onto the bottom rope, so that my dick was even with her mouth, and pushed myself between her lips. She welcomed the taste of herself that surrounded my dick and swirled her tongue as I gently fucked her mouth. It couldn't last long, because I was too anxious to be back inside of her, but I just wanted to feel that warm mouth while she was posted up in the ring.

When I pulled back and settled back onto the floor, I replaced my dick with my tongue, kissing her deeply and passionately. Her lips were tremulous, the whiplash of the way I kept changing things up making her feel nervous and excited.

That was how I wanted her.

Pushing myself back into her core, I broke the kiss long enough to hiss at how right it felt. "Mine," I whispered to myself, basking in the fact that she was mine. Then I kissed her again, holding her to me, and thrusting fast and hard like I promised in the beginning.

She responded immediately and came quickly, like her body had been on edge and waiting for the moment I finally let her come. She was squeezing so hard; I could feel her almost pushing me from her body. But we both knew I loved a good fight, so I pushed back inside of her harder and harder until I was releasing my cum into her in waves.

It seemed everlasting and with a new feeling of contentment that I had never felt with her before. Knowing we had jumped the hurdles, passed the roadblocks, and found our way to each other was making our connection that much sweeter.

I knew we still had a few more punches headed our way, but it felt freeing knowing that no matter the outcome, I had realized that she was worth the fight–just like Cam had hinted.

"I think Cam knows."

"What?" She rose up from where she was lying on my chest, running her fingers across the plane of my abs. We were lying together in my bed where we had been all week.

Rhys saw us come in after we had left the gym Tuesday night, and he left me a text Wednesday morning telling me that since I seemed to be better, and out of my funk, he was going to go back to Miami full time. Which made me happy since I was starting to think there was someone he wanted to go home for.

I had been too messed up in the previous few weeks to ask him about it, but I wasn't blind. He was distracted in his own way, and his trips back to Miami seemed more frequent than doctor appointments would have needed.

With that being said, Charleigh and I hadn't left the comfort of the penthouse since. But it was now Sunday, and I had to get back to work to prepare for our rematch with Chicago in our home stadium the next weekend.

"Cam?" Charleigh brought me back to earth with his name and I remembered I had started that conversation.

"Oh, yeah." I pulled her back to my chest and ran my other hand through my hair. "I don't think he realizes it's you, but he knows I've been suffering from some sickness that only a woman could invoke."

She giggled and pinched my side, making me laugh as well. It was unlike me, to laugh so unrestrained, but I had been doing it all week. At times, I didn't even recognize myself. I had been so focused on my career throughout my life that I had never had moments like I had with Charleigh.

We had ordered in food, watched movies, had a lot of sex, and now we were getting ready to do something I never dreamt I would ever do. We were about to watch football together.

Chicago didn't have the weekend off and I had told her I wanted to watch their game. I expected her to complain and not want to but instead she added, "Their quarterback used to play for Seattle, so it will be like a homecoming for him. I wonder how that will affect his pass game since Seattle's defense is well attuned to his nuances?"

I had pulled her underneath me and fucked her hard after that, turned on by her insight. I knew a lot of women who sincerely loved football, but I knew very few women who knew the small details of the game that made it so strategic and fun. I was going to miss the game when I inevitably lost my job, but I would be content knowing it was for her.

"As much as I hate to say it," I pulled the covers from her before I got hard again thinking about her football mind. "If we watch the game in bed, I will end up fucking you the whole time."

She laughed again and made her way out of bed, strutting naked toward my bathroom. One look over her shoulder, inviting me to join her, was all it took for me to kick out of bed and chase her down. She sped up and squealed as I gave chase, catching her and picking her up into my arms.

When I settled us both into the shower, letting the water fall down over the top of us, and looked into her happy eyes, I knew I was in love.

Deeply.

Fiercely.

Intensely.

Dangerously.

We had confessed as much when we settled the feelings between us at Bobby's, but we had yet to repeat the words. I was tempted then and there, to make sure she knew that even though we were emerging out of our bubble and getting back to work that week, that I loved her and was positive I always had.

I held back, knowing there were still things we had to overcome, but I was confident that if we could get through the season, everything else could be handled between our careers. All I had to do was keep Richard away from her, and with a few false promises, I knew it could happen.

What I wasn't prepared for was how intense my feelings for Charleigh had become. So strong that I didn't get past the next game before I threw the white flag in on my career.

charleigh

LEVI and I had both had to get back to the real world, which meant we could no longer spend every waking moment together. We did, however, manage to sneak in moments with the help of people who knew what was happening.

Bobby was now in the loop, and unbelievably enough, he was incredibly supportive. He encouraged me to leave early on a couple of nights that Levi had off, and on Friday, he once again made sure the gym was empty by the time Levi got there.

"Thank God this place doesn't have cameras," he huffed as he slid me the key that night. I stayed quiet, but laughed to myself at how many times I thought that same thing.

Bobby had decided to spend the money that Levi gave him to redo the ring and make it worthy of the kind of fights he hoped to host in the future now that Sisco had made a name for himself, and the gym.

All I could think about was how much I couldn't wait to christen the new mats with Levi once they were installed. Hell, sex with Levi was just about all I thought about anymore. Maybe because it was still new, or maybe because for the first time in my life, sex was more than pleasure, it was love.

I loved Levi so damn much, and with the support of my mom, and even Jesse, I knew loving him was the right thing to do. My dad had died a long time ago, and she never remarried, much less dated. But she had that sparkle in her eye that told me she had found love, believed in it, and was happy I had found it.

Levi and I agreed to keep things a secret for a while. In fact, we both insisted. But when it came to Richard, he wanted me to trust him and let him handle it. I had no plan but to keep avoiding Richard at all costs, so I gave Levi the lead on whatever he wanted to do.

I trusted him.

It was finally game day again and I was feeling rested after being away from the field for two weeks. I met with my fellow officials like I always did, but instead of being anxious and worried about where Levi was and what would become of the day, I allowed myself to feel relief that I knew he was there.

My phone buzzed in my pocket, and I reached into my black uniform slacks to pull it out and check my messages.

> If you see my hands in front of my crotch, just know I am hiding how hard you make my dick when I see you in that uniform.

I smiled and glanced toward Levi, trying not to look too obvious. When I saw him, his eyes were focused on his team, yelling every so often to a player with his fingers interlocked in front of his pants.

I shook my head and looked around the stadium, trying to throw anyone that had been watching off the obvious scent that I was looking at Coach Peyton. But I did take a minute to text him back.

Thank goodness my pants are black since they're the only thing hiding how wet I am for you.

No panties?

Too much trouble for the post-game interview I have planned.

Fuck, I have to take a cold shower.

I looked up to see him jogging off the field toward the corridor before his team was set to leave the field. Was he really headed to a shower?

If I knew him, probably. I just wished so badly that I could join him.

"How are ya?" I heard Richard ask behind me.

I turned around and noticed he was talking to the entire officiating crew, but his eyes were zeroed in on me.

"Good," I faked a smile. Things were never good when he was around.

"Can I talk to you for a minute, Ms. Wright?" he asked. The other officials looked confused, but they nodded goodbye as Richard walked a few paces away for privacy. I followed him, but I didn't want to, and even though I knew Levi had left the field, I still looked around for him like he could save me.

"How was your weekend off?"

"Good," I said again, as if it was all I knew how to say.

"Coach Peyton told me you two had a chat."

My eyes widened, because Levi told me to trust him, but I didn't actually know what was said or what to do. So, I chose to nod, neither confirming nor denying, just showing him I was listening.

"I trust you know what is at stake now."

With that, he walked away casually, sliding his hands into his overpriced suit pants. I started looking around for Levi, but he was still in the locker room. The team started making their way down there, too, so I knew Levi would put his phone up for the rest of the game.

Still, I tried to text him.

> Richard told me you two chatted, but I have no idea what that meant. Just that I apparently know what is at stake now. I trust you, but I should know what I am up against. What does he know?

There was never a response and eventually, I had to get ready for kick off. I was standing in the center of the field with the other officials getting our last pregame talk from Martin. Then we broke and made our way to our positions–me jogging directly toward Levi.

He and Cam Nichols were standing side by side, looking at a play chart, but Levi glanced up at me as I got closer. He started with a small nod of acknowledgement, but I must have still had the worry in my eyes because he did a double take and stopped listening to Cam.

He took two steps forward and met me by the line, jerking his headset from his head. "Are you okay?"

I looked up at Cam who heard Levi's concern, and even though he told me he thought Cam knew something, he didn't know it was me, and we agreed to keep it that way for a while longer.

"Good Coach," I nodded. "How are you today?"

He caught my overly pleasant response for what it was and looked over to Cam. He didn't seem to care. Before getting back to Cam and the game, he turned back to me. "Don't worry about him, tell me if you need me."

I nodded. "All good."

He knew it wasn't, but he let it go as the kickoff was moments away. I turned and got into position and the game started without any more worry.

For the entire first quarter, I could hear Levi behind me barking into his headset and yelling at the players about positioning and effort. He was in his coaching zone and now that I wasn't afraid to admit it, listening to his coaching was incredibly sexy. He was an amazing coach, and the guys responded to him like a father figure.

By the second quarter, the Jets were close to scoring and I was on the goal line. On a quarterback sneak, I couldn't see Cam cross the goal, so I called it down on the half yard line, making them kick a field goal instead. Levi was irate, thinking his quarterback had the touchdown, but he didn't throw his red flag. He chose to chew me out instead.

"He had that, Stripes," Levi yelled.

"You should have challenged it if you thought so," I replied while walking down the sideline, back to midfield. "We've been over that already."

"I shouldn't have to use it for that obvious of a play." His voice was high, and his anger was real. He was Coach Peyton at that moment, not my Levi, and I loved every second of it. I almost smiled, hoping that when we got back to his place later, we found out that I did blow the call and he took it out on me in the bedroom.

"You think this is funny?" he yelled again, completely oblivious to my train of thought.

"Throw the red flag, Coach," I repeated and kept walking.

He threw his headset and his clipboard, stomping like he was having a tantrum. When he settled himself down, he settled back behind me and barked some more. "Get your glasses on, Stripes."

I ignored him, but he made me momentarily forget about Richard. He wasn't even thinking of me as his girlfriend, or lover–

whatever we were. I was back to being his coaching nemesis. The referee that he stood closest to and got every single piece of his wrath.

The next play, I called pass interference on his defense, and again, he was in my ear, fuming more than I had ever heard him.

"There was a whole foot in between them!"

"Pay attention!"

"Fucking idiot!"

On his final insult, I couldn't help it, I looked back at him and smirked. His insults should have pissed me off, but I just got more and more turned on. Richard was a long-lost memory, and by halftime, all I could think about was Levi spanking my ass again because we didn't agree on the calls.

You need some therapy, Charleigh, I thought to myself.

I sat in my locker room alone during halftime, knowing Levi wouldn't show up to fuck some sense into me. We had agreed we wouldn't take that risk since we had started sharing a bed almost every night.

When I made my way out, back into the corridor, I fell alongside Levi as he too made his way out. I didn't risk giving him a look, just walked while he listened to someone talk on the other side of him.

But right before we left the corridor, he stopped me, and the look on his face made my heart fall to a painful death. Something had changed, something was wrong.

I started to ask what was up, but he stopped me from speaking until the final player passed us to get back to the field.

Then he ran a hand down his face and looked me in the eye.

"I can't do this."

levi

I WAS DOING GOOD, staying in my coaching zone and separating my personal life and my football life. I was treating Charleigh like any other referee, and I meant every word that I said in the moment.

I even started the game feeling good about where things were with Richard. I had asked Charleigh to trust me, and even though I didn't have an elaborate plan, I thought I had saved her for a while at least.

During the pregame meeting, I asked to speak to him alone, and told him that I had spoken to Ms. Wright. I told him that she was falling for my charm, and that if he promised not to scare her, I knew I could have her under our thumb by the end of the next few games.

None of it was true. I just wanted him never to speak to her again while I got Art involved in an investigation. But Richard just patted my back and told me he was glad I finally realized the opportunity we had with her under our control. He promised to let me take it from there.

But when I saw my phone at halftime, and the message that Charleigh had left me, I knew I wasn't going to last another second. I meant what I told Charleigh before–I was the only one who could talk to her like that. I was irate that he dared to speak to her after I had told him not to.

It was a test. He was confirming with her that I really did talk to her. And I guess she played along enough for it to work. But that wasn't the point. He scared her; he had no business getting near her. I wanted to kill him for even saying hello to her.

"I can't do this," I confessed to her at the end of halftime.

Her eyes darted around, wondering who had heard us, but it didn't matter anymore. I wasn't going to make it till the end of the game now that I knew Richard did not hold up his end of the deal.

He never would.

He would continue trying to intimidate her and I couldn't let that happen.

"What do you mean?" she asked, her voice shaking.

I realized she took my comment wrong, immediately worried I meant I couldn't do us anymore. After the way I was yelling at her, I should have been more specific.

"Fuck," I pulled her behind the wall so no one could see us and wrapped my arms around her. "I just got your text from before the game. I made a deal with Richard, but he had to never speak to you. He broke that deal within the hour, and now all I want to do is kill him. So, I can't do this, baby. I can't even coach the second half of the game."

"Just try," she took her hands to either side of my face. "I can handle Richard. I just wasn't sure what to say. But it's okay."

I shook my head over and over again with her hands still on my face. "It's taking everything I have. I need to hit something."

"Okay, then we'll go to the gym after the game. You can hit me."

I smiled a little, and instantly calmed a little at her words. Not that she was hilarious, and not that I would actually hit her. But for the first time in as long as I could remember, I didn't feel alone. Rhys was a great babysitter for a while, but nothing beat the feeling of knowing Charleigh had my back.

It helped me refocus, and I nodded to her that I would try. We kissed quickly and chastely, then I ran from the corridor and out with the team as they warmed back up after halftime. Charleigh came out a few minutes later and joined the officials and everything started off smoothly.

Even the third quarter was good. Charleigh would look back every once in a while and check on me but I was fine. Calmed and collected as much as I could get. But I never forgot about Richard sitting in his air-conditioned box, looking down on us and thinking he needed to keep speaking to Charleigh.

I wasn't the same man that I was when the season began. My priorities had changed, and I was excited by how good it felt to feel those changes in my heart. I was doing okay, making it play by play, and looking forward to taking my girl home after the game.

Then sixty-seven entered the game for Chicago.

I eyed him, remembering the video I played over and over again of him messing with Charleigh. I thought about the look in her eyes after the game in Chicago, and how upset she had been at how nastily he had treated her. Not that she couldn't handle it, but the fact was, that she shouldn't *have* to handle it.

The night we spent together on the rooftop, she told me about what he had done, and that he had touched her. But the entire game, he had been on the sidelines across the field being the least of my worries. Now he was playing on our side of the field, and combined with my anger over Richard, I was back to wanting to explode.

I stayed quiet behind Charleigh, calling the game and coaching the best I could, but I watched every single thing sixty-seven did. As long as he stayed in line, I would be fine. Or I hoped I would be.

But he couldn't do that.

He eventually found himself being pushed over the sideline, and cut between the players to find his footing. He had dropped the ball so there was nothing to hand off to Charleigh, and no reason he had to even go near her.

But he did.

Sliding past me, oblivious that I was watching him, he made his way next to Charleigh and inconspicuously leaned into whisper something to her. Everyone else would have assumed it was nothing–coincidence or just a normal word with the referee. I wasn't everyone else and I saw it all.

I couldn't hear what he said, but I saw Charleigh's face morph to anger. I saw the fight in her rise up and her willing herself not to respond. She looked back at me, probably just wondering if I noticed, but when our eyes connected, I felt her pain.

She wanted respect.

She wanted dignity.

She wanted courtesy.

And I wanted her to have whatever she wanted.

My feet started moving before my brain connected with what our plan was. There really wasn't even a plan, I was moving on instinct. I couldn't confront Richard at that moment, but I could take care of sixty-seven easily.

When I passed by Charleigh, she saw in my eyes that I was in fighter mode. She didn't even try to stop me, just watched me pass by, and out onto the field. Everyone watched on, wondering what I was doing. Because they were all lost to what had happened, no one even tried stopping me. If I knew my players as well as I thought I did, they wouldn't try stopping me even if they did know. In fact, they would be lined up helping me.

"Sixty-seven," I yelled when I was in the middle of the field. I saw his name on his back, but I refused to use it.

He turned around and looked confused–everyone was confused. What was the head coach doing on the field in the middle of the game? He smiled at me like I was going to ask for his autograph, but instead, I grabbed onto the face mask of his helmet and pulled his face to mine.

"Don't you ever touch, or speak to her again. Do you understand me?"

He looked confused at first, but then figured out who I was talking about. His eyes got wide as flags started flying from the other referees. I knew I would be ejected from the game for approaching a player with the intent to kick his ass, but it was like I told Charleigh at halftime–I couldn't do it anymore.

Without letting him respond, and before I got pulled off of him, I yanked his mask again with my left hand pulling his helmet off. Then I swung my fist on my right, landing a blow directly in his jaw.

By then, there were people everywhere, pulling him from me and pushing me away from him. I had hoped to get more than one punch in but his team took him farther and farther away as mine did the same.

The head referee predictably ejected me from the game, and I walked straight to the sideline to get my headset. I didn't bother placing it on my ears, just spoke into the microphone to the coaches in the booth.

"Get Richard to my office as soon as possible."

I threw the headset down and walked to my office, waiting for Richard. If he thought he was coming to do damage control, he would be sadly mistaken.

There was nothing to control.

Nothing to even talk about.

There was just one thing on my mind.

Richard was my next victim.

charleigh

LEVI COULDN'T HOLD his anger in anymore.

I watched as he took sixty-seven's helmet off and punched him in the jaw. He would have gotten in more than one if the players and coaches weren't separating them. Martin was throwing flags everywhere, but looked completely confused and taken aback by Coach Peyton's actions.

He glanced at me, silently asking if I knew how it all started. I nodded because I did know, but it wasn't going to be the answer Martin thought he was going to hear.

Once Levi walked from the field, and toward the corridor, Martin approached me and I forced myself to shake off the shell shock.

"What the hell was that about?" Martin asked. I am sure he expected me to say something about sideline tension, or sixty-seven pushing, or talking shit. But Levi was living in the moment with his true feelings on his shoulders and I wanted to do the same.

"It was me," I confessed. "Sixty-seven passed by me and told me that my pussy belonged in a cheerleading skirt."

"What?" Martin yelled, starting to look around for Chicago's villain. "Where the fuck is he?"

"I'm sure he's in the tent." I was referencing the medical tent the teams had on the sidelines to check out players quickly. "I don't know what to do."

Martin looked back at me and winced. "Coach Peyton heard him?"

"I guess so." I honestly didn't know what he knew for sure. I just knew he saw my disgust and sadness, then snapped and headed onto the field.

"The league will handle his punishment for charging a player on the field. But after the game, I need you to file a complaint form."

"Okay," I whispered. "I'll do that."

It wasn't the time to tell Martin about Levi and me, but I was tempted. I just wanted to leave the game and go find him. I wanted to make sure *he* was okay.

"Are you okay to continue?" Martin asked, sensing my discomfort.

I started to say I was because that was what I should have said. I was strong enough to deal with the players and the coaches, so in any other circumstance, I shouldn't have been rattled. But knowing Levi was alone and dealing with a fire he had inside himself since halftime, I wanted to go to him.

Martin didn't let me answer, he just nodded toward the corridor, indicating I should head off the field. He didn't have to tell me twice. I started running in a sprint, down the corridor and toward the player's locker rooms where I knew Levi's office was.

Levi wasn't in the office; he was pacing the hallway in front of his door like a caged lion. When I started making my way toward him, he looked up and paused, relief settling in his expression at seeing me.

Before I made it to him, the door on the other end of the hallway slammed and Levi spun around to see who it was.

Richard.

His smug expression was bouncing between Levi and me as he approached. He was foolishly alone, not realizing that Levi was a fighter. I was thankful he hadn't found out yet about Levi's extracurricular activity because that made him easier to get to.

No one to protect him.

Levi was waiting for Richard to approach, but I started running toward both of them, passing Levi so I could be the first to get to Richard. Levi had already taken care of one of my problems, now I wanted to help him with the other.

Richard wasn't expecting me to get aggressive. I was sure he saw me as nothing but a weak little girl. But I was also a fighter. I pulled my arm back right as I approached him and swung so hard he never saw it coming.

He fell to the ground and I got over the top of him, taking my left hand to the other side of his face. "You think you can control me?" I yelled. "You think I will just bow down to you because you wear fancy suits and have a lot of money?"

Levi was behind me, his hands in his pockets and looking down at us. Richard was blocking his face from my assault, but looked to Levi for help. "Can you get her off of me?"

Richard was about to learn–quicker than we had planned–that Levi wasn't working for him anymore.

"She deserves more, Richard. You're lucky she's choosing violence."

Their interaction, and Levi's words, made me pause, and I backed away to let Richard get up. He shuffled until his back hit the wall of the hallway and then made his way to his feet.

"How am I lucky for that?" Richard squeaked, sounding like the pathetic man he was underneath the facade.

"Because if she didn't, I would have, and I hit much harder."

"You're fired," Richard yelled at Levi, then turned to me. "And you will never officiate in this league again."

I nodded in agreement. I may never officiate in the league again. My lifelong dream would only ever be a short stint in reality. But if I was going to be treated the way Richard treated me, and the way sixty-seven treated me, then it was no longer my dream.

Richard backed away from us as Levi took an aggressive step forward. He was trying to get through the door and back to where other people were, so he felt safer. His fear made me feel a sense of satisfaction.

Now he knew how it felt.

Once he was out the door, it was only a matter of time before the cops came for us. We would probably both be arrested for assault, but it was a thousand percent worth it.

Levi grabbed my hand and led me into his office where he locked us in. We both had blood on our knuckles, and neither of us knew whose blood it was, but that didn't stop us from embracing.

"I'm sorry baby, I tried." Levi was whispering into my ear, apologizing for not even lasting a day when it came to "fixing" our on the field issues.

"The truth feels better."

He pulled back and looked into my eyes. "I'm sorry that falling for you meant ending your dreams so quickly."

"It didn't, Levi." I pushed my hands up to the side of his face, careful not to get blood on him. "It just showed me I had another dream, and now it has come true too."

Just as we started kissing, a knock on the door broke us apart and as I had predicted, the police were there.

We didn't fight it that time. We knew what was coming, and we knew we would be out of there by the end of the day.

"See you tonight?" Levi winked as the cops read him his rights and cuffed him like a hardened criminal.

"I'll come to you," I smiled, allowing the cops to cuff me as well.

I wasn't upset that things didn't go as planned, or that Levi had lost his cool on the field. In truth, it was the first time someone besides Bobby and my mom stood up for me and made me feel like I didn't have to fight as hard as I had my entire life.

I wasn't alone, and I felt contentment knowing that whatever came of our careers, we had chosen each other, and the rest didn't matter. It blew my mind how much had changed in such a short time, but when I really thought about it, it wasn't such a short time at all.

From the moment I first met Levi, well over four months before, I knew he was meant for me. We may have gone on a wild path to get to each other, but we couldn't deny that it was always meant to end the way it did.

levi

ART FLEW into Atlanta the day after everything went down on the field with Chicago. But instead of being worried about my attack on sixty-seven, he was more concerned with the behind the scenes attack that Charleigh had unloaded on Richard.

As he probably should have been.

I had my lawyer bail both Charleigh and me out of jail before the game was even over. He had arranged for me to have a car service take me home, but I added that he needed to discreetly make sure Charleigh was in that car with me.

We sat in the backseat, hand in hand, as we went to her apartment first to get whatever she needed for the next few days. She also spent the drive on the phone with her mom and Bobby, assuring them everything was fine.

Rhys told me he would fly back in to help me over yet another hump, but I told him no need, that Charleigh and I were okay, and as long as we were together, it would be fine.

We spent that night soaking in my bath together, massaging and cleansing the day from our bodies. I wanted to take her to bed and make love to her until we could no longer remember who

Richard was, but just being with her the way we were was equally as satisfying.

We sat in robes on the couch after the bath and ate takeout. We dared to turn on the sports channels to see what everyone was saying, but they were just as confused as they should have been.

Still, everyone was oblivious to how much Charleigh and I meant to one another.

No one knew Richard had been attacked, or that Charleigh had been arrested, but they were able to deduce that I went after sixty-seven because of what he said to her. Apparently, I was a hero, but my stomach churned at that mention, because I knew the truth.

That I had failed her before, and didn't deserve accolades for finally manning up and punching sixty-seven.

Charleigh noticed my self- loathing and slid into my lap to kiss me. Kissing never stayed kissing with us, and eventually, I was holding her by the thighs and driving my dick into her from where she straddled over the top of me.

The next morning, we were both separately summoned to the Omni hotel where Art had set up an office to determine what had happened, and what he should do about it. Instead of going separately, though, we decided to show up together.

The Omni was just a block from my penthouse, so we walked together, holding hands and soaking in the sun from the Monday afternoon rays. When we walked into the hotel, we were immediately corralled by a few NFL employees and taken to Art's makeshift office.

He was surprised to see us both walk in, and even more surprised we were hand in hand. But we refused to start over and hide again. It was too much for us to defend ourselves, and our actions, without being open about how we felt.

Richard may have had the power to fire me from the Jets, but Art had the power to kick me out of the NFL. It was important to me that he knew Charleigh was my priority, and that if it came down to it, I wanted her to keep her job and I would head back to coaching college football.

"Well, this is a surprise," he motioned to our hands as we walked in. "But not really."

I furrowed my brows and looked at Charleigh before going back to Art. "Seriously?"

"Sit..." he trailed off, motioning to the chairs that sat in front of his temporary desk.

We did but kept our hands together.

"So, let's see..." he thumbed through some paperwork that sat before him. "Coach Peyton, you charged a player on the opposite team and assaulted him in the middle of the field. You were arrested, but there were no charges filed by anyone, so your arrest was nulled this morning. Richard Elder, however, fired you, yet he won't tell me why."

I nodded, considering that Richard wasn't telling Art because he knew the truth made him look bad.

"Richard has been threatening Charleigh since the beginning of the season, and my girl here is a fighter, so she snapped and let Richard know she wasn't going to take it anymore. Who was I to stop that?"

Art's eyes were wide with disbelief, so Charleigh and I told him the entire story, right down to when we met in New York, to when we decided fighting the attraction was no longer worth it. We both told him that we knew we were done with the NFL but needed to see this through. We couldn't pass up what was most likely our only chance at being with our soulmate.

"So, this isn't an affair? This is the real deal?" he asked us.

Charleigh smiled and nodded. "Yes sir. I'm so sorry I disappointed you and the NFL before my first season was ever complete. I know as one of the first female referees in the league, you expected more from me, but I think what really came of it was the need, going forward, to educate the players, coaches, and owners on how to treat the female officials that you bring into the league. Also, while I am sorry things didn't go as planned, I am not sorry for falling in love with Levi."

Art leaned back in his seat as the look on my face told him how much I loved hearing her say she was in love with me. He looked between us, and then tossed his pen onto the desk in resolve.

"There is nothing I can do about Richard. As the owner of the Jets, he gets the final say so about who he employs, and who works inside his stadium. However, as the commissioner, I can make sure you both are employable by the NFL. Richard will not want to face a board of NFL owners with his head on a platter because of how he treated you, Ms. Wright. I assure you he will drop the charges and sweep this so far under the rug, it will be as if it never existed."

I started to speak but Art stopped me so he could keep going. "I know that is not what either of you wanted to hear, but remember... I work for the owners in managing the league, not the other way around. What I can do is use this as a reason to implement training for the rest of the league so that it is less likely to happen again."

"That is completely acceptable, Mr. Mixon," Charleigh interjected. "Thank you for that. As more women are brought into the league, it will be important that they know there are guidelines, and consequences for being treated the way I have been."

"I have already sent a team to San Francisco to interview Patty Lamb, our other female referee. I want to know if she has experienced anything similar and was just afraid to come forward."

We nodded and looked around, ready to leave now that we knew our fate. But did we know our fate? Art had been vague and indirect.

"Okay," he stood by way of dismissing us. "I am going to be in Las Vegas for the game next month, so I will see you both then."

We both looked at him disbelieving, assuming he had lost his mind. "Sir, I was fired."

"I assumed I was, too," Charleigh added.

"Richard needs you more than you need him. He will get you back on that field, or I am willing to bet the entire team protests until you return. He doesn't want them to know why you were fired, remember? He only incriminates himself if he has to explain."

"But I'm not sure I want to work for him, knowing that I see him for who he is now."

Art waved me off and laughed, "You want to coach your team though, so you will. Besides, you have all the power, and I expect you to use it. Enjoy it. Protect it. Don't forget that the worst Richard can do is actually fire you for being a shitty coach, and that isn't the case. And in the end, if he lets you go after the season, you are no worse for wear. As for you, Ms. Wright, you've been through enough. You don't need to be punished for falling in love. All I ask is that you two continue to keep things professional and away from the field, and by the end of the season, things will work themselves out."

On that note, we stood in shock and left Art. We walked quietly across the park and back to my penthouse, still not sure how we were going forward.

As Art predicted, Richard texted me and told me to get back to work. I started to text him something about how far he could shove his phone up his ass, but before I could hit send, I had a knock on my door.

I opened up and saw Ty and Giselle asking to come in.

"Hey Coach," Ty gave me a half hug while Giselle wrapped me into a huge hug. "Where's the ref?"

I smirked, not knowing how he knew but glad he did. "In the bedroom changing, she'll be right out."

"So, you coming back tomorrow?" Ty looked desperate, having just been forced to send his own brother to jail. I was his family, the team was his family, and I remembered instantly that I couldn't leave him if I could help it.

I picked my phone up and erased the message to Richard, choosing to give him a thumbs up instead. Then I looked up to Ty and nodded. "Yep, I'll be there."

charleigh

I DISEMBARKED from the plane in Las Vegas, anxious to get to Levi. He flew with the team, and I flew solo, which was the way it was supposed to go.

Richard had decided to take a step back to let things cool down and allow Levi to coach the team without his interference. Chicago's number sixty-seven was released from the team for being a shitty player, so that dish was served better than I could have planned.

The entire Jets team knew about Levi and me, but everyone kept it close to their chest. We made sure that while in the eye of the world, we were nothing more than referee and coach. But when the clock hit zero, we rushed to find privacy and make up for all the ugly things we said to each other on the field.

Levi and I had decided that after the next season, he was going to move back to college coaching while I remained refereeing in the NFL. At first, I protested, but he said he felt like he was being called to set an example for the younger guys. Molding them into strong and intelligent men was something he took pride in, and knew for them, it started at the college level. Plus, he wanted to be more open with our relationship, and that was impossible as long as we were both at the NFL level.

I had fallen more in love with Levi as the days went on. We were moving fast and hard... always fast and hard.

When I got to the hotel, I immediately went to the room number Levi told me was his, and foregone my own room that the league was supposed to arrange for me. When Levi opened the door, I flew into his arms and wrapped my legs around him, grinding myself on him the way I loved doing.

He kissed me back, fiercely, and we almost fell onto the couch, anxious to tear each other's clothes off. But before that happened, we heard someone clear their throat. I leaped from Levi in a hurry and he looked around the room like he had forgotten we weren't alone.

Levi's room was huge, not just an average hotel room, but a suite. Some familiar faces, and some new faces, were staring at me.

"Um," I looked at the people staring back at me, smirks covering all their faces. "Shit."

Cam Nichols and Tyson Black were sitting with their arms wrapped around their girlfriends, both of whom I had gotten to know well in the last few weeks. But they weren't the only people there.

Kace Jackson was on the other side of Ali and Cam, holding Ali's hand while Cam held the other. Then there was Giselle and Ty, tucked into each other as well. The rest of them were all new faces, but not unfamiliar.

Cam spoke up to start introductions. "Hey, LJ," he called me LJ for line judge, and it kind of stuck. "I invited my sister and her jackass boyfriend, Chase Turner. Chase, Becca, this is Charleigh, or as I like to call her, LJ."

I nodded and Levi wrapped an arm around me to soothe my anxiety over the new people. Chase stood up and motioned to another couple sitting next to them. "Then I decided to invite my friend Ethan and his girl Madison. So Ethan, Madison, this is Charleigh."

I nodded again, this time acknowledging the new names that Chase had introduced me to. I had seen every single one of them on TV and the sports channels. I knew exactly who they were, but it was surreal seeing them in person.

"So," Levi kissed my head again. "This kind of turned into a party."

I smiled, because it was the first time we had people to hang out with who knew about us, and weren't worried about the dynamics of our controversial relationship.

"Ty was just telling us about his ballet performance coming up for Christmas. I got us tickets," Levi laughed, while Ty rolled his eyes.

"We are all going," Chase added. "I wouldn't miss Ty in a tutu to save my life."

Everyone laughed and nodded their agreement.

"Y'all ready?" Kace stood, taking Ali with him, and away from Cam.

"Let me just change," I stopped everyone from moving. I didn't know what the plans were, but I was excited to go out. "I smell like an airplane."

"And I need to help her," Levi winked, chasing me to the bedroom of the suite.

"We are barging in and watching if you take too long, Coach," Ty yelled as Levi shut the door.

"Don't worry, little guy," Levi yelled back. "I can get her off before halftime is over."

He slammed the door and laughed, picking me up and throwing me onto the bed. We shed my clothes quickly, anxious to get to each other after a whole day apart.

"They better not know about halftime," I moaned as he smiled against the bare skin of my thigh.

"They don't," he confirmed. "But they wouldn't be shocked... or even mad about it."

"How do you know?"

"Because every single one of those guys is in love, just like I am. They would do the same thing for their girl if she wanted them to."

Love was a word that Levi and I started saying with more intent and meaning after our meeting with Art at the Omni. There were no theatrics involved, he just pulled me into his arms in bed that night and told me he loved me, along with telling me good night.

As soon as I returned his sentiment, we were both asleep, but we never stopped expressing how much we loved one another.

Levi had taken all my clothes off and worked his way up my thigh until he started lapping at the wetness between my legs. He teased, nipped, and bit me before I started coming so hard, I was sure our company heard me calling his name in the next room.

With them threatening to come in, and with plans I didn't even know we had, Levi rose up and unbuckled his pants, shoving into me hard and quick. He fucked me deep, making the moaning I had during my orgasm feel like puppy love.

Nothing was better than having him inside of me, making me feel full and leaving my body in goosebumps from head to toe. "You better come baby, or we'll *be* the show tonight. They all have tickets and will walk right in here to see how I treat the ref."

The thought of them walking in and seeing me so undone was erotic, and it was just the image I needed to send me over the edge. Levi followed, emptying himself inside of me with his head tipped back and biting his lip in pleasure.

"Okay, Coach," Cam's voice came through the door. "We took

notes, and you win. But now we gotta go if we're gonna make the fight."

My eyes widened and I rushed to the bathroom to clean up. Levi followed me and helped me throw new jeans on while simultaneously trying to run a brush through my hair.

"Where are we going? What fight?"

"Grishom vs. Holt," he said with a smile. "The fight you wanted to see. Did you forget it was this weekend?"

"Yes!" I yelled, so excited that he remembered. "I love you, Levi," I almost cried.

Before he opened the door to the room, he stopped me and tucked some hair behind my ear. "I love you too, baby. And you know I am always up for a fight with you," he whispered and placed a soft kiss on my lips. "With you, for you, over you, and any other way you want to fight."

Levi

"WITH RICHARD ELDER selling the Jets, it's safe to assume you will want to continue as head coach for the foreseeable future?"

"Yes, sir," I nodded to Mr. Mixon. "But I won't stand in the way of Charleigh doing whatever she wants to do. So, I'm prepared to step down, and the new owners of the Jets are aware of that."

Mr. Mixon leaned back in his chair and sighed. We were in New York, in his office, and it reminded me of my last off-season trip when I met Charleigh. She flew with me since she had her own meetings, but we hadn't had a chance to talk about what happened with her yet.

"That isn't going to be necessary. As long as there is never a question that you both are honorable, then I will overlook the conflict of interest, with one exception. The playoffs. She will not be allowed to referee any postseason as long as the Jets are in the playoffs."

"That seems fair, considering most referees can't officiate in the postseason for their first five years."

"Precisely. Should she want a post-season spot in five years, you two will have to decide what your future holds. Until then, keep things professional. Do not flaunt your relationship on the field."

"Yes, sir." Knowing we were going to both be okay, I was anxious to get to her.

"When I met with her earlier, I expressed how proud I was of her. She handled herself well. Falling into a relationship with the head coach of one of the teams was *not* what should have happened, but I'm not crazy enough to think you two had a choice. Despite all the threats and drama that was created with her presence, she called good games, made good calls, and handled herself with grace."

"She's a professional, Mr. Mixon. It's one of the things I love about her."

"Well then, you two have a lot to celebrate. Enjoy the rest of the off-season, and I will see you both in August. You have a lot of work to do with the new owners. They seem like a good family."

Nodding, I stood quickly, anxious to get back to the hotel. I was tempted to call Charleigh on my way, but I held back, wanting to see her face when we finally shared our good news.

The taxi I took barely had time to stop before I jumped out and walked toward the bar. When I entered, I started a beeline for her as she sat with her legs crossed and a martini at her fingertips. Her head fell back, laughing at something the bartender said, and I paused, soaking in the look of her being so happy. It was a stark contrast to the first time I saw her sitting there.

Over a year before, she sat in that exact seat, looking nervous and withdrawn. At the time, I thought she had been stood up, or had her heart broken. But now I knew she had just been anticipating her interview with the NFL. It was a life-changing weekend for her.

For us.

Instead of sidling up next to her, I decided to sit at the table I was at the first time I saw her. The waitress came by and I ordered a whiskey, then settled back in the seat to watch her. The bartender was still telling her something that had her laughing and distracted, but once her head came back down and her eyes scanned the room, she found me.

At first, her brows rose up and then furrowed, confusion settling on her face. But then she smirked and shook her head slightly as she realized what I was doing. When she raised her glass to me and took a sip, I took my cue and stood, making my way to where she was sitting.

"Is this seat taken?" I asked, pointing to the stool next to her.

"No," she smiled, playing along.

Licking my lips, I reached my hand out for her to shake and debated on what name I was going to use to introduce myself. My first instinct was to tell her my name was Brett, and to play the role exactly the way I had before. But then I remembered all those nights I had stroked my own cock, wishing I knew what my real name had sounded like on her lips.

"I'm Levi," I decided to tell her, changing my only regret in our history.

Surprised, she smiled again, and placed her hand in mine. "Charleigh. Nice to meet you."

"Can I buy you another drink?"

"Tequila and lime," she nodded.

I motioned for the bartender to grab us another drink, and she nodded without having to take our order. When I turned my attention back to Charleigh, she was still smiling at me with a knowing look in her eye.

"So, Charleigh, what brings you to New York?"

"Work," she said simply, then took a sip of her new drink. "You?"

"Same. Work."

"But that isn't why you came over here, is it?"

"Not at all," I growled, getting closer to her ear. "I came over here hoping you'd want to join me in forgetting about work."

"I definitely want to forget about work, Levi."

Grabbing her hand, I flipped her wrist over and ran my finger up the inside of her forearm. Goosebumps rose on her skin and I leaned in close enough to whisper in her ear.

"I bet I can make you come in seconds, Charleigh. You're not going to be able to move after I'm finished with you."

"I hope you mean that, Levi. I'm not the kind of woman that likes to teach a man how to touch her."

"Finish your drink. Then let me take you upstairs."

"You're not wasting any time," she smiled. The first time we met, it took a little longer to get to where we were at that moment, so not only was she saying the truth, but she was also repeating what she had said that first night.

"I'm anxious to know what you taste like."

I knew what she tasted like. She tasted like a mix of *heaven* and *mine*. My cock was hard with anticipation and I wasn't sure how much longer I would be able to keep up the act.

"Mr. May," Charleigh moaned into my ear. "I'm going to call you Mr. May."

She was definitely off-script, and I laughed, realizing that we were once again in New York in May. "As long as I am also Mr. June, July, and August."

"You're Mr. Forever," she sighed, then let her head fall onto my shoulder.

The game was over, and both of us were too anxious and ready to be alone upstairs. I pulled her head up and grabbed her chin, putting my lips close to hers. "Let's get out of here, Stripes."

She slid from her stool and started walking toward the elevator. I watched her hips sway for a minute before she looked over her shoulder like a siren. Then I was practically running to catch up to her, not bothering being the smooth and put together man I was the night we met.

Brett no longer existed.

Charleigh didn't love Brett; she loved Levi. And Levi was the man who would chase her, fall to his knees for her, and be the name she screamed every time she came.

ANOTHER 6 MONTHS LATER

Charleigh

"Are you blind, Ref? His hands were all over him."

"They were both battling for the ball, Coach."

"No, the fuck they weren't. Number 53 had his hands in Black's mask."

"Step back," I urged, trying to get Levi out of my face so I could get in position for the next play.

"You're gonna cost us the game," he yelled again. "I'm not backing off until you start calling a good game."

My back was turned to him, and I tried not to laugh at how irate he was. Levi Peyton was next-level angry, barely registering that he was yelling at the same woman that sucked his dick that morning. Not that I wanted it any other way.

We had done well separating our work life and home life. Very few people knew about our relationship, and since I was in my second year, I was no longer assigned to do games primarily in Atlanta. The league had spent the off-season making sure there were facilities in all thirty-two stadiums for both of the league's female referees.

In fact, I was only scheduled to work two of Levi's games all year, and only one of them was in Atlanta. It was a primetime game against Chicago. Luckily, number sixty-seven was no longer on the team, so we didn't have to worry about Levi charging him on the field again. But we did have to be wary of the entire world watching his every move.

After the next play, Atlanta's offense came off the field and Cam Nichols stood behind me while the field reset. He was one of the few that knew how involved Levi and I were, and he was laughing as Levi continued yelling at everyone around him.

"See what you did, Stripes? You stirred him up and made him mad."

Smiling, I placed my whistle in my mouth to make it harder to read my lips. "He'll get over it."

"You two have a strange relationship," Ty added, making Cam laugh again.

"Get the fuck away from her," Levi yelled, making them mumble, '*Yes Coach,*' and back away.

The game had restarted with Atlanta on defense, and when I called a first down for Chicago, Levi lost his cool again. He didn't bother waiting for me to walk back to the sideline; he ran onto the field and got in my face.

"Where the fuck did you get this uniform? Footlocker? Spirit? Does your boyfriend know you're fucking us this hard?"

My stoic demeanor faltered, and I laughed, making Levi back up and look at me. His face made me realize he had no idea what he was saying. He was just shouting in anger.

"Don't bring my boyfriend into this. He'll kick your ass. He's always looking for a fight."

Levi growled and walked around me toward the sideline. He spent the rest of the game grumbling behind me, but no longer gave me shit for any calls. When the clock hit zero, he jogged toward the middle of the field to shake hands with the other coach and then ran off the field quickly.

It took me a little longer to chat with my fellow referees and wish them a good week. But when I got to my locker room, I sank onto the couch and took a deep breath. It was definitely harder calling a game with Levi behind me now that we were in a committed relationship. Not that I was mad at how angry he was, but more like how turned on I was by that vein wanting to pop out of his forehead. The way he threw his hat and stomped past me like he was ready to swing at me.

Fuck, I was crazy, but that was who we were. It worked for us.

When I got up to head to the shower, I noticed a note on my mirror. I grabbed the small piece of paper and read Levi's handwriting.

Leave the uniform on, Stripes. Wait for me.

Smiling, I shook my head and looked up at the TV screen in the corner. He was in the middle of his press conference, and I was originally supposed to head home and meet him there.

Instead, I decided to lie down and do as he asked, staying in my uniform and waiting for him. There was no telling how long it took, but I dozed off and woke up to Levi caressing my cheek.

"Hey Ref. Wake up, baby."

Sitting up, I yawned while he pulled me into his lap. My head laid on his shoulder, but he jostled me back up.

"Wake up. I want to show you something."

"Why did I have to leave my uniform on? It's itchy."

"Because it's hot, and I love it when I get to take it off of you."

"I'll let Footlocker know they did good."

Levi snorted and stood up, making me stand next to him. "Yeah, yeah," he pulled my hand and led me to the door, then out into the corridor. "We all know my finest moments are not on that field."

"Then why are we headed that way?" I nudged him.

"Because there was one thing that bothered me during the game, and I want to discuss it."

"Levi," I whined, tired and ready to go home, "Can't we get naked in a bath and talk about it? We can watch the film, and if I got the call wrong, I'll let you get a hit in next time we spar."

"No, we are going back to the scene of the crime," he insisted, pulling me harder onto the field.

The stadium was completely empty, and it made me wonder again how long I had been asleep. With very few lights on, it was almost ominous to be out there but equally exciting.

"Right here," Levi pointed to the grass. "This is where it happened."

"What happened?" I tried to remember, but it had been a long game, and Levi was mad about most of it. How was I supposed to know what he was talking about?

"This is where I asked if your boyfriend knew you were fucking us so hard."

Laughing, I covered my mouth and watched the amusement in his eyes. "You gonna apologize?"

"Fuck no," he snorted. "But the next time I go on a tirade..." he trailed off, reached into his back pocket, and went down onto one knee. "I want to be sure I can use the word fiancé."

A black box appeared, and my eyes widened with shock. Of all the ways I thought Levi might propose, this wasn't it. Especially after an Atlanta loss.

"You don't know how close I came to turning around earlier and getting on one knee for you in front of everyone. The ring was in my pocket the whole game, and even when I wanted to throw you back through the front doors of Eye Solutions, I also wanted to beg you to marry me. When I asked about your boyfriend, you were standing right here, and I knew it had to be the last time we used that word. I don't want to be your boyfriend, Charleigh. Fuck, I don't even want to be your fiancé. I want to be your husband. So please marry me, baby."

"Oh my God, yes," I cried.

Levi bit his lip as he pulled the ring from the box. He slid it onto my finger from his knee and then kissed my hand. I heard the shutter of a camera going off and looked to the side to see Cam and Ty clapping and smiling. Then they gave a quick wave and ran off the field.

"I asked them to take a few pics," Levi explained. "Wanted photographic evidence of you in that uniform and me on one knee."

"So I can use it against you next time you get grumpy?"

"So you always know that no matter what, I love you, and I will choose you first. Always."

"I already know that," I smiled as he lifted me into his arms and spun me around.

"Now," he growled and put his forehead to mine, grabbing my neck. "Let's go home. I'm going to fuck you until you apologize for blowing those calls."

"You'll be fucking me all night." It would be a cold day in hell before I apologized for doing my job.

"I know," he laughed. "But I'm up for the fight."

afterword

This book is dedicated to those who helped me fight because it was written while I was in the hospital. Not only the doctors, nurses, and staff, but my family...my husband, kids, and parents. Also, to my friends, who stepped up and helped me in every way possible! I love you all so much.

Writing a head coach was my favorite. The words and ideas flowed and seemed endless. Levi practically wrote himself, and I want to bring these two back...somehow, somewhere... not just in Reckless Goals (where Levi helps Rhys find love) but their own extra story. I just have to wait for that spark of inspiration.

Love to all,

Katie

about the author

Katie is a hopeless romantic, a proud mother of two, a devoted wife, and a die-hard baseball fan. She resides in Florida where she loves beach days and boat life.

There is always more to a Katie Rae book than what you think! She loves making us think while also making us swoon. You always think you know, but you have no idea, and that is what makes Katie Rae books so special.

Join the fun in Katie Rae Reader Group and sign up for Katie Rae's Newsletter!

Also, www.katieraebooks.com is now LIVE. Check out merch, extras, events, book information, signed paperbacks, and MORE!

If you loved this story, please consider leaving a review! These reviews are so important for authors and help us be seen.

Goodreads

Bookbub

Amazon

also by katie rae

The GAMES Series (interconnected standalones)

The Games We Play

The Lies We Tell

The Love We Make

The Way We Dance

The Way We Fight

Men of the Military (complete standalones)

Ranger

Raptor

RECON

Rogue

Miami Inferno FC Series (Interconnected Standalones)

Reckless Goals

Scoreless Nights

Twisted Assist

The Boys of Summer Novella

Pretty Boy

Man of the Month Club Novella

Love Bites

Another One Bites the Dust

Silverbell Shore Series (standalone)

Now and Then

Co-Write with Zoey Drake (standalone)

Dirty Monsters

Website Exclusives

The Christmas Playbook (A GAMES Christmas novella)

Manny Christmas (Standalone Christmas novella)

Railbird (A ROGUE short story... free download)